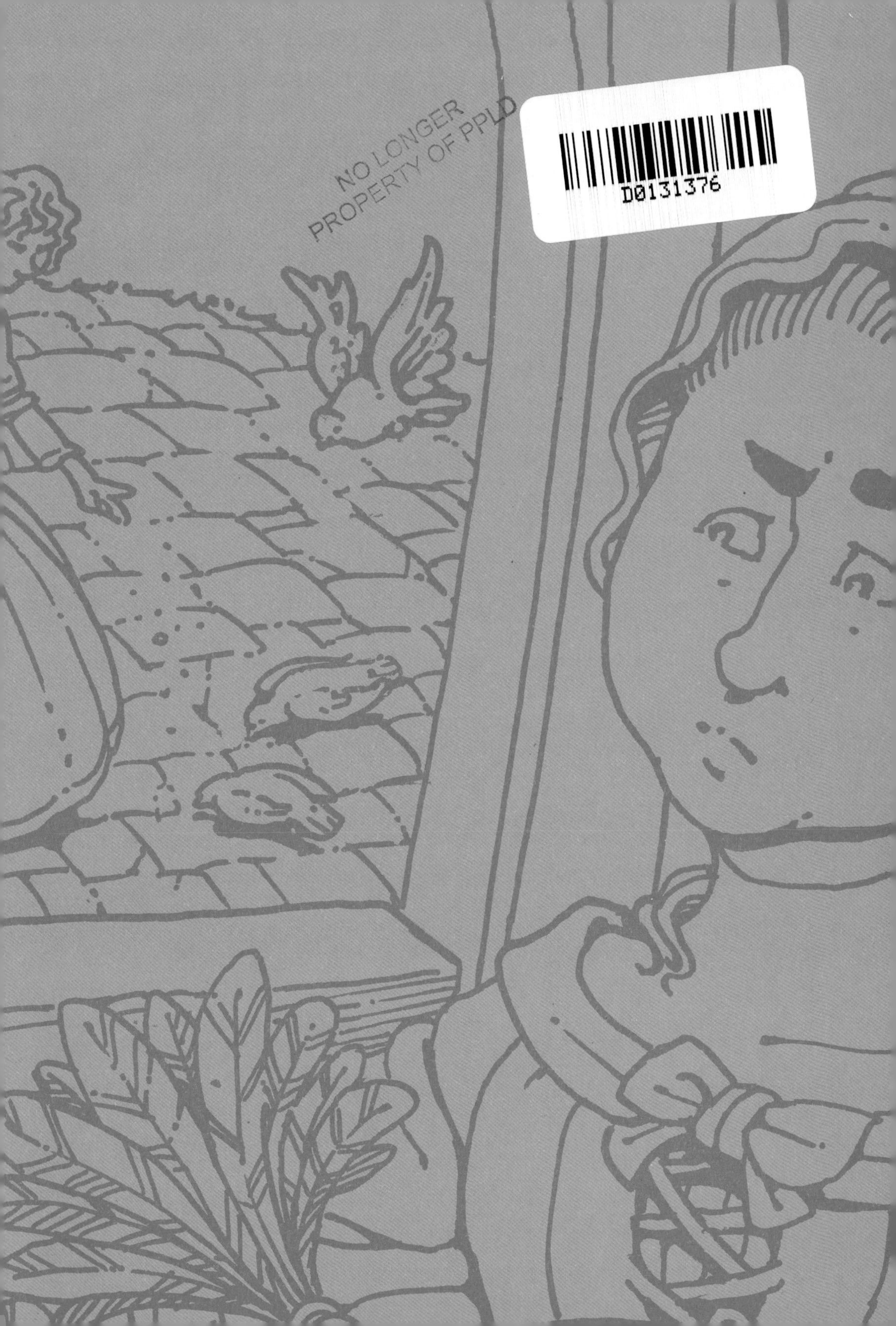

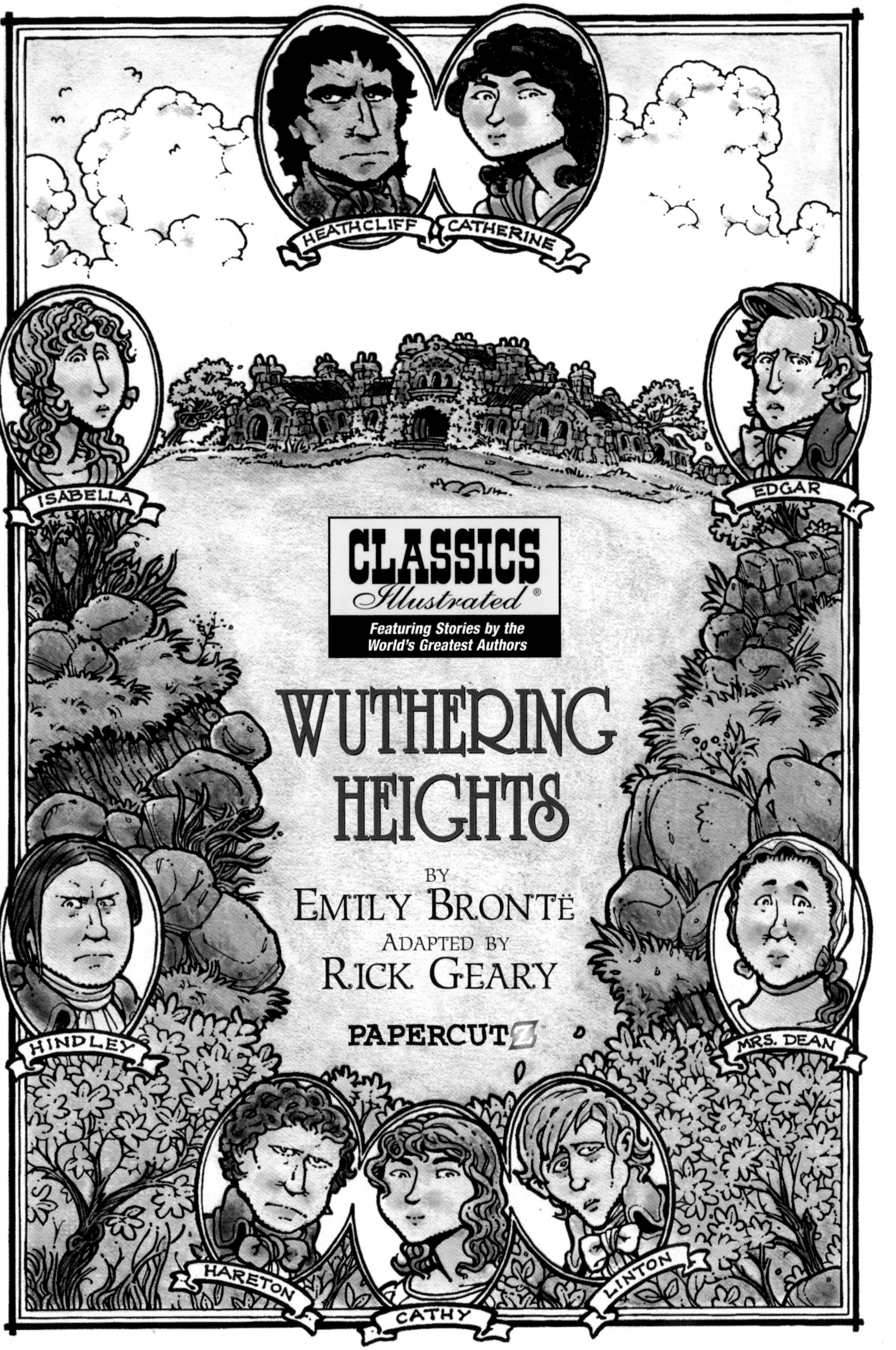
HEATHCLIFF
CATHERINE
ISABELLA
EDGAR
HINDLEY
MRS. DEAN
HARETON
CATHY
LINTON

CLASSICS *Illustrated*®

Featuring Stories by the World's Greatest Authors

WUTHERING HEIGHTS

BY
EMILY BRONTË

ADAPTED BY
RICK GEARY

PAPERCUTZ™

CLASSICS ILLUSTRATED GRAPHIC NOVELS AVAILABLE FROM PAPERCUTZ

#1 "GREAT EXPECTATIONS"

#2 "THE INVISIBLE MAN"

#3 "THROUGH THE LOOKING-GLASS"

#4 "THE RAVEN AND OTHER POEMS"

#5 "HAMLET"

#6 "THE SCARLET LETTER"

#7 "DR. JEKYLL & MR. HYDE"

#8 "THE COUNT OF MONTE CRISTO"

#9 "THE JUNGLE"

#10 "CYRANO DE BERGERAC"

#11 "THE DEVIL'S DICTIONARY AND OTHER WORKS"

#12 "THE ISLAND OF DOCTOR MOREAU"

#13 "IVANHOE"

#14 "WUTHERING HEIGHTS"

COMING DEC. '11 #15 "THE CALL OF THE WILD"

CLASSICS ILLUSTRATED graphic novels are available only in hardcover for $9.95 each, except #8-15, $9.99 each. Available from booksellers everywhere.

Or order from us. Please add $4.00 for postage and handling for the first book, add $1.00 for each additional book. MC, Visa, Amex accepted or make check payable to NBM Publishing. Send to: Papercutz, 40 Exhange Place, Ste. 1308, New York, NY 10005

www.papercutz.com

CLASSICS *Illustrated*®

Featuring Stories by the World's Greatest Authors

70th Anniversary Edition

CLASSICS Illustrated® Featuring Stories by the World's Greatest Authors

#14

WUTHERING HEIGHTS

By Emily Brontë

Adapted by Rick Geary

PAPERCUTZ™

New York

The only novel written by Emily Brontë, **Wuthering Heights** was published in 1847, attributed to one "Ellis Bell." Pseudonyms were common literary disguises of the era, especially for women writers who aspired to the serious consideration given their male counterparts. As was usual, argument raged about the author's real identity. A year earlier, the three Brontë sisters – Charlotte, Emily, and Anne – had published a poetry collection credited to "Currer, Ellis, and Acton Bell." In England's literary circles, it was widely believed that the Brontë sisters and the "Bell brothers" were three and the same. Nevertheless, the single credit served up cause for controversy: Which "Bell" was really which Brontë sister? Further complicating the matter were some readers who held that all three pseudonyms actually belonged to Charlotte; still others suggested that the "Bell" pen names were unrelated to any of the Brontës, and served instead to camouflage some other writer's identity. Upon Emily's death in 1848, she still had not been officially credited with authorship of **Wuthering Heights**. That finally came in 1850, when the novel's second edition appeared, bearing her name. Critics of the time responded indifferently to **Wuthering Heights**, comparing it unfavorably with Charlotte Brontë's *Jane Eyre* and many regarded the novel as excessively morbid and violent. Eventually, a gradual critical reassessment – championed by Charlotte – resulted in recognition of Emily's genius and acknowledgement of **Wuthering Heights** as a singular masterpiece. It represented a radical departure from the Victorian tradition of the novel. While other contemporary works were thickly populated, **Wuthering Heights** was narrow in scope; while others relied upon complicated, often convoluted, action, **Wuthering Heights** was free of contrived scenes, its drama resulting from the clash of wills. A rich meld of romance and realism, it abounds with passion, turbulence and mysticism – "the horror," observed Charlotte, "of great darkness."

Wuthering Heights
By Emily Brontë
Adapted by Rick Geary
Wade Roberts, Original Editorial Director
Alex Wald, Original Art Director
Production by Ortho
Classics Illustrated Historians – John Haufe and William B. Jones Jr.
Associate Editor – Michael Petranek
Jim Salicrup
Editor-in-Chief

ISBN: 978-1-59707-249-6

Printed in China
August 2011 by New Era Printing LTD
Trend Centre, 29-31 Cheung Lee St.
Rm.1101-1103, 11/F, Chaiwan

Distributed by Macmillan.

First Papercutz Printing

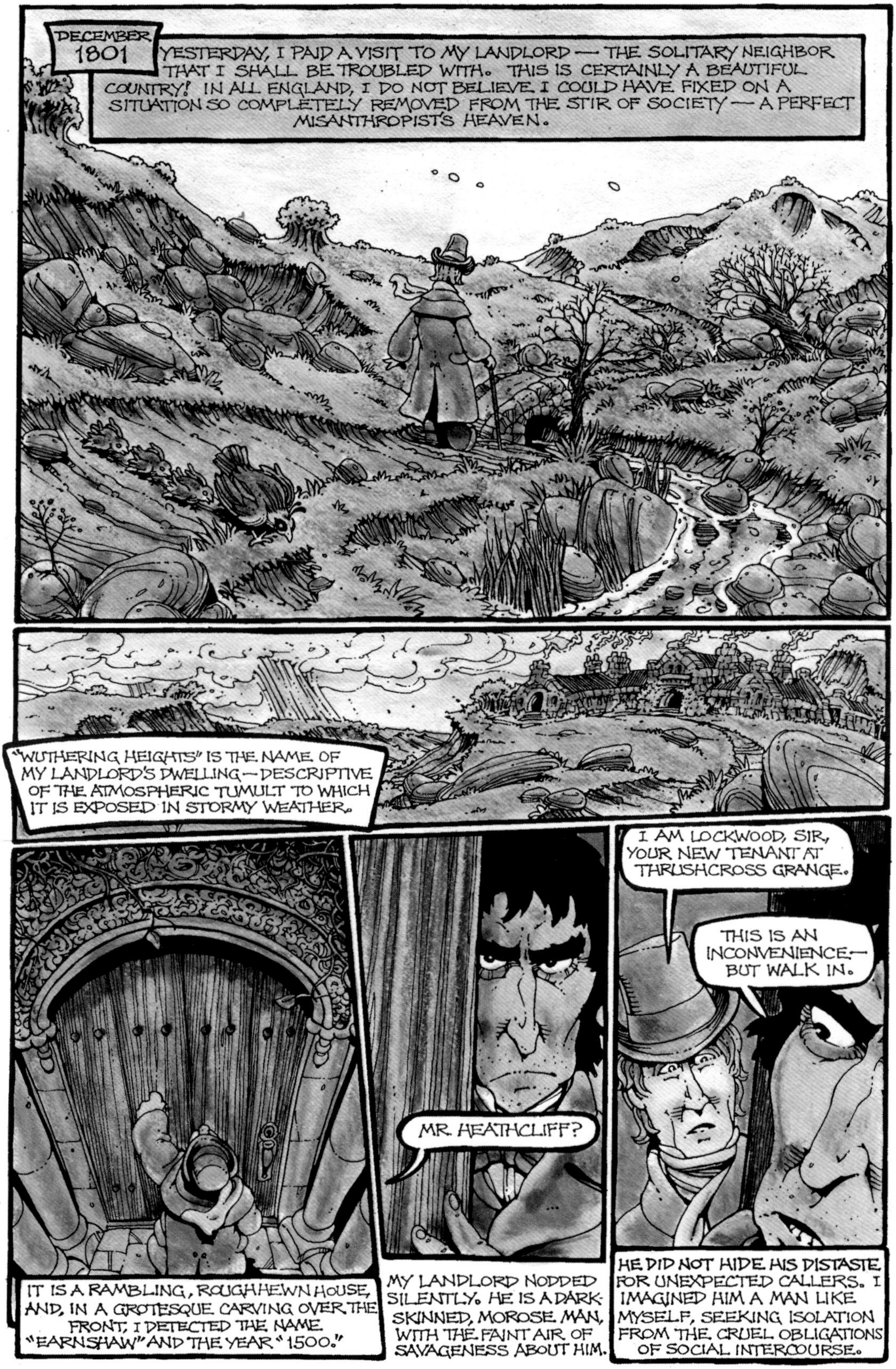
DECEMBER 1801
YESTERDAY, I PAID A VISIT TO MY LANDLORD — THE SOLITARY NEIGHBOR THAT I SHALL BE TROUBLED WITH. THIS IS CERTAINLY A BEAUTIFUL COUNTRY! IN ALL ENGLAND, I DO NOT BELIEVE I COULD HAVE FIXED ON A SITUATION SO COMPLETELY REMOVED FROM THE STIR OF SOCIETY — A PERFECT MISANTHROPIST'S HEAVEN.
"WUTHERING HEIGHTS" IS THE NAME OF MY LANDLORD'S DWELLING — DESCRIPTIVE OF THE ATMOSPHERIC TUMULT TO WHICH IT IS EXPOSED IN STORMY WEATHER.
IT IS A RAMBLING, ROUGHHEWN HOUSE, AND, IN A GROTESQUE CARVING OVER THE FRONT, I DETECTED THE NAME "EARNSHAW" AND THE YEAR "1500."
MR. HEATHCLIFF?
MY LANDLORD NODDED SILENTLY. HE IS A DARK-SKINNED, MOROSE MAN, WITH THE FAINT AIR OF SAVAGENESS ABOUT HIM.
I AM LOCKWOOD, SIR, YOUR NEW TENANT AT THRUSHCROSS GRANGE.
THIS IS AN INCONVENIENCE — BUT WALK IN.
HE DID NOT HIDE HIS DISTASTE FOR UNEXPECTED CALLERS. I IMAGINED HIM A MAN LIKE MYSELF, SEEKING ISOLATION FROM THE CRUEL OBLIGATIONS OF SOCIAL INTERCOURSE.

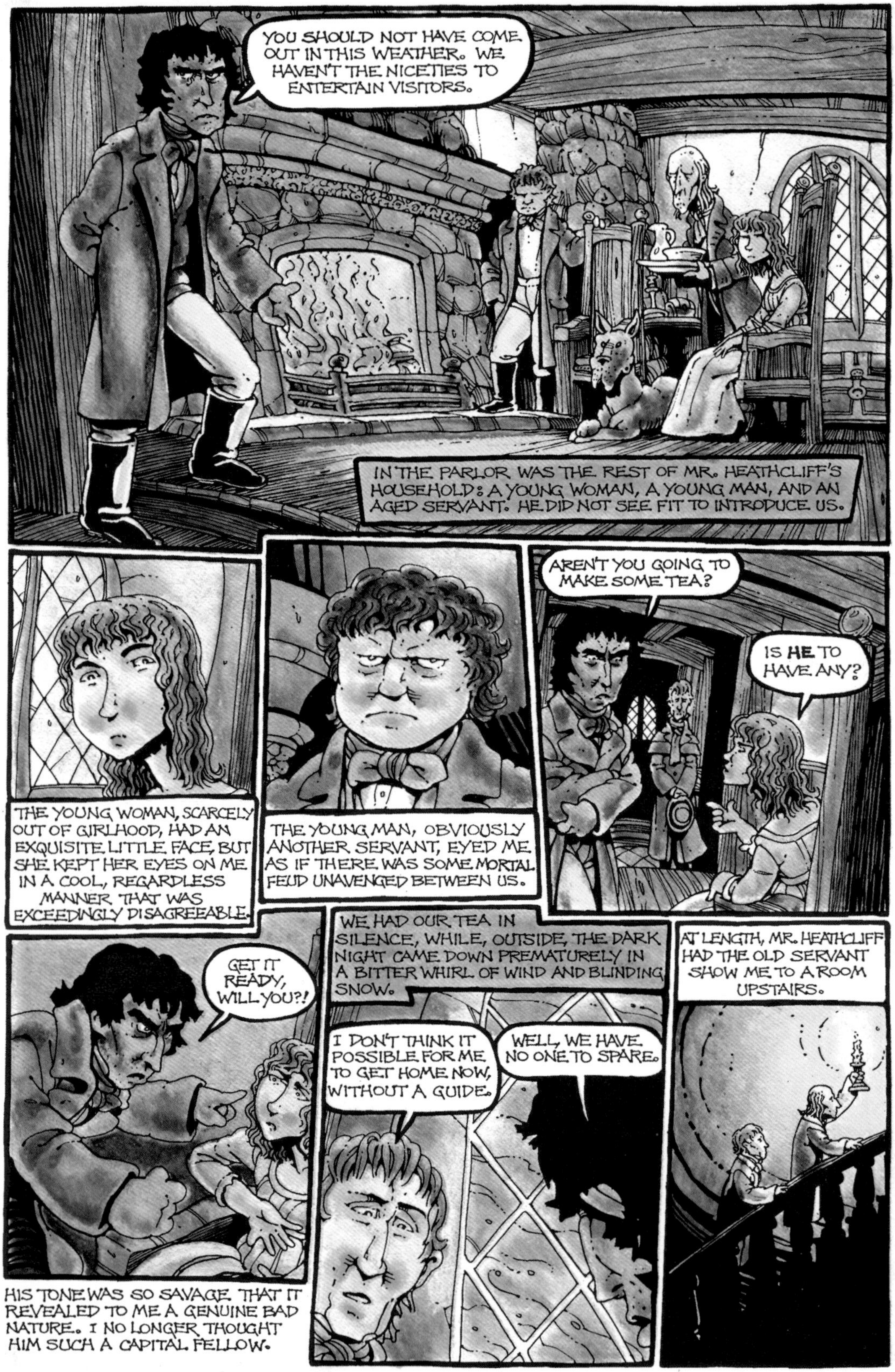
YOU SHOULD NOT HAVE COME OUT IN THIS WEATHER. WE HAVEN'T THE NICETIES TO ENTERTAIN VISITORS.
IN THE PARLOR WAS THE REST OF MR. HEATHCLIFF'S HOUSEHOLD: A YOUNG WOMAN, A YOUNG MAN, AND AN AGED SERVANT. HE DID NOT SEE FIT TO INTRODUCE US.
THE YOUNG WOMAN, SCARCELY OUT OF GIRLHOOD, HAD AN EXQUISITE LITTLE FACE, BUT SHE KEPT HER EYES ON ME IN A COOL, REGARDLESS MANNER THAT WAS EXCEEDINGLY DISAGREEABLE.
THE YOUNG MAN, OBVIOUSLY ANOTHER SERVANT, EYED ME AS IF THERE WAS SOME MORTAL FEUD UNAVENGED BETWEEN US.
AREN'T YOU GOING TO MAKE SOME TEA?
IS **HE** TO HAVE ANY?
GET IT READY, WILL YOU?!
HIS TONE WAS SO SAVAGE THAT IT REVEALED TO ME A GENUINE BAD NATURE. I NO LONGER THOUGHT HIM SUCH A CAPITAL FELLOW.
WE HAD OUR TEA IN SILENCE, WHILE, OUTSIDE, THE DARK NIGHT CAME DOWN PREMATURELY IN A BITTER WHIRL OF WIND AND BLINDING SNOW.
I DON'T THINK IT POSSIBLE FOR ME TO GET HOME NOW, WITHOUT A GUIDE.
WELL, WE HAVE NO ONE TO SPARE.
AT LENGTH, MR. HEATHCLIFF HAD THE OLD SERVANT SHOW ME TO A ROOM UPSTAIRS.

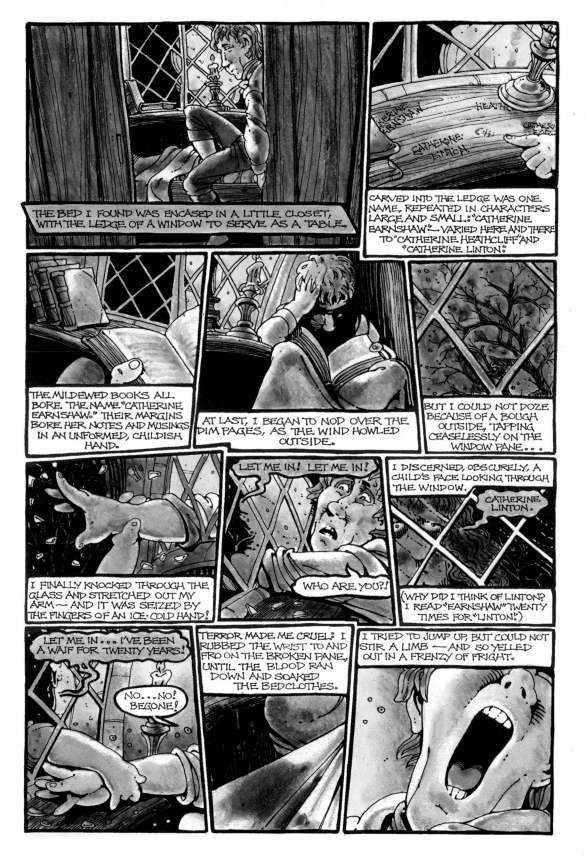

THE BED I FOUND WAS ENCASED IN A LITTLE CLOSET, WITH THE LEDGE OF A WINDOW TO SERVE AS A TABLE.

CARVED INTO THE LEDGE WAS ONE NAME, REPEATED IN CHARACTERS LARGE AND SMALL: "CATHERINE EARNSHAW"— VARIED HERE AND THERE TO "CATHERINE HEATHCLIFF" AND "CATHERINE LINTON."

THE MILDEWED BOOKS ALL BORE THE NAME "CATHERINE EARNSHAW." THEIR MARGINS BORE HER NOTES AND MUSINGS IN AN UNFORMED, CHILDISH HAND.

AT LAST, I BEGAN TO NOD OVER THE DIM PAGES, AS THE WIND HOWLED OUTSIDE.

BUT I COULD NOT DOZE BECAUSE OF A BOUGH OUTSIDE, TAPPING CEASELESSLY ON THE WINDOW PANE...

I FINALLY KNOCKED THROUGH THE GLASS AND STRETCHED OUT MY ARM— AND IT WAS SEIZED BY THE FINGERS OF AN ICE-COLD HAND!

LET ME IN! LET ME IN!

WHO ARE YOU?!

I DISCERNED, OBSCURELY, A CHILD'S FACE LOOKING THROUGH THE WINDOW.

CATHERINE LINTON.

(WHY DID I THINK OF LINTON? I READ "EARNSHAW" TWENTY TIMES FOR "LINTON"!)

LET ME IN... I'VE BEEN A WAIF FOR TWENTY YEARS!

NO...NO! BEGONE!

TERROR MADE ME CRUEL: I RUBBED THE WRIST TO AND FRO ON THE BROKEN PANE, UNTIL THE BLOOD RAN DOWN AND SOAKED THE BEDCLOTHES.

I TRIED TO JUMP UP, BUT COULD NOT STIR A LIMB — AND SO YELLED OUT IN A FRENZY OF FRIGHT.

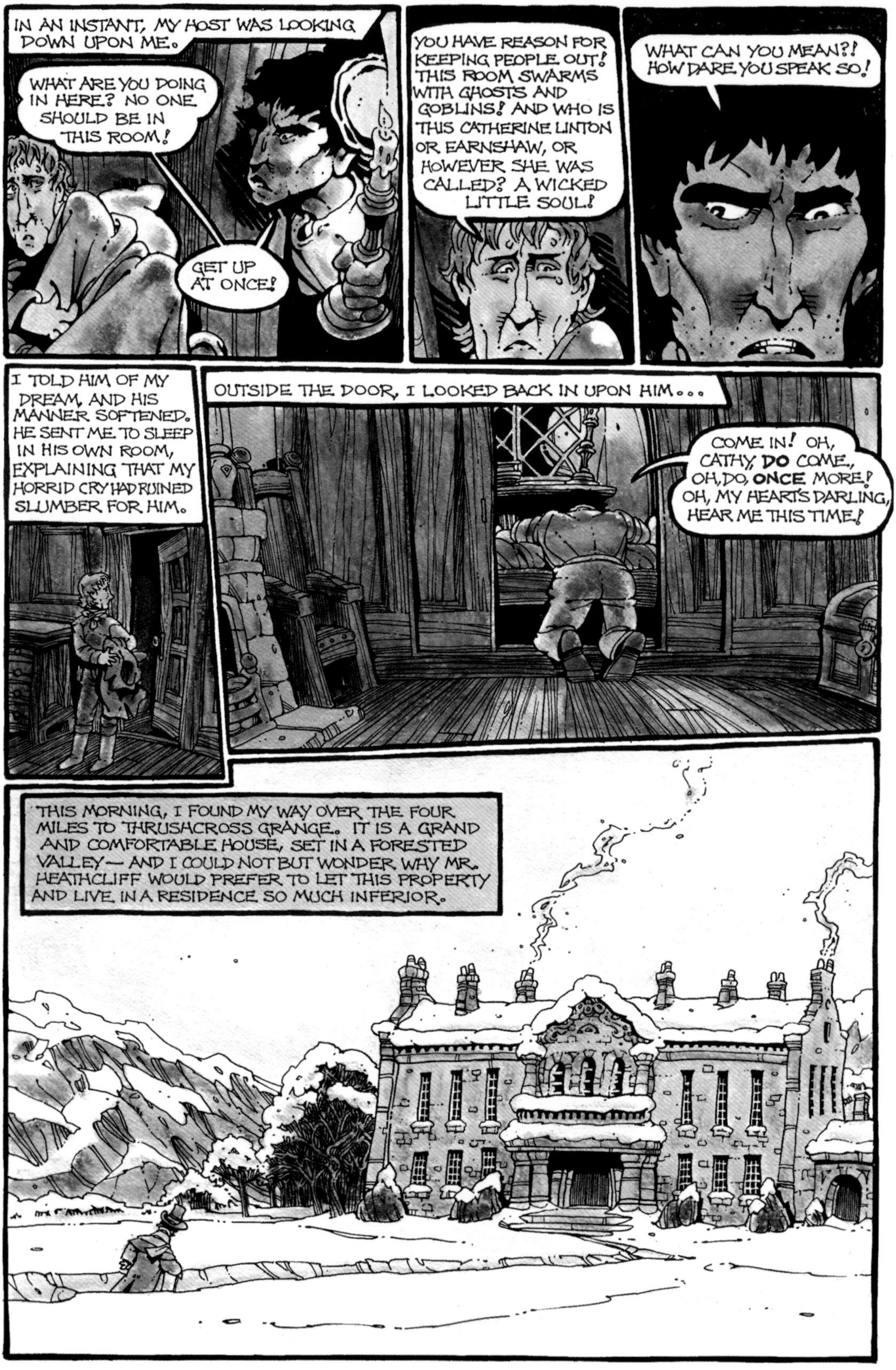
IN AN INSTANT, MY HOST WAS LOOKING DOWN UPON ME.
WHAT ARE YOU DOING IN HERE? NO ONE SHOULD BE IN THIS ROOM!
GET UP AT ONCE!
YOU HAVE REASON FOR KEEPING PEOPLE OUT! THIS ROOM SWARMS WITH GHOSTS AND GOBLINS! AND WHO IS THIS CATHERINE LINTON OR EARNSHAW, OR HOWEVER SHE WAS CALLED? A WICKED LITTLE SOUL!
WHAT CAN YOU MEAN?! HOW DARE YOU SPEAK SO!
I TOLD HIM OF MY DREAM, AND HIS MANNER SOFTENED. HE SENT ME TO SLEEP IN HIS OWN ROOM, EXPLAINING THAT MY HORRID CRY HAD RUINED SLUMBER FOR HIM.
OUTSIDE THE DOOR, I LOOKED BACK IN UPON HIM...
COME IN! OH, CATHY, **DO** COME. OH, DO, **ONCE** MORE! OH, MY HEART'S DARLING, HEAR ME THIS TIME!
THIS MORNING, I FOUND MY WAY OVER THE FOUR MILES TO THRUSHCROSS GRANGE. IT IS A GRAND AND COMFORTABLE HOUSE, SET IN A FORESTED VALLEY— AND I COULD NOT BUT WONDER WHY MR. HEATHCLIFF WOULD PREFER TO LET THIS PROPERTY AND LIVE IN A RESIDENCE SO MUCH INFERIOR.

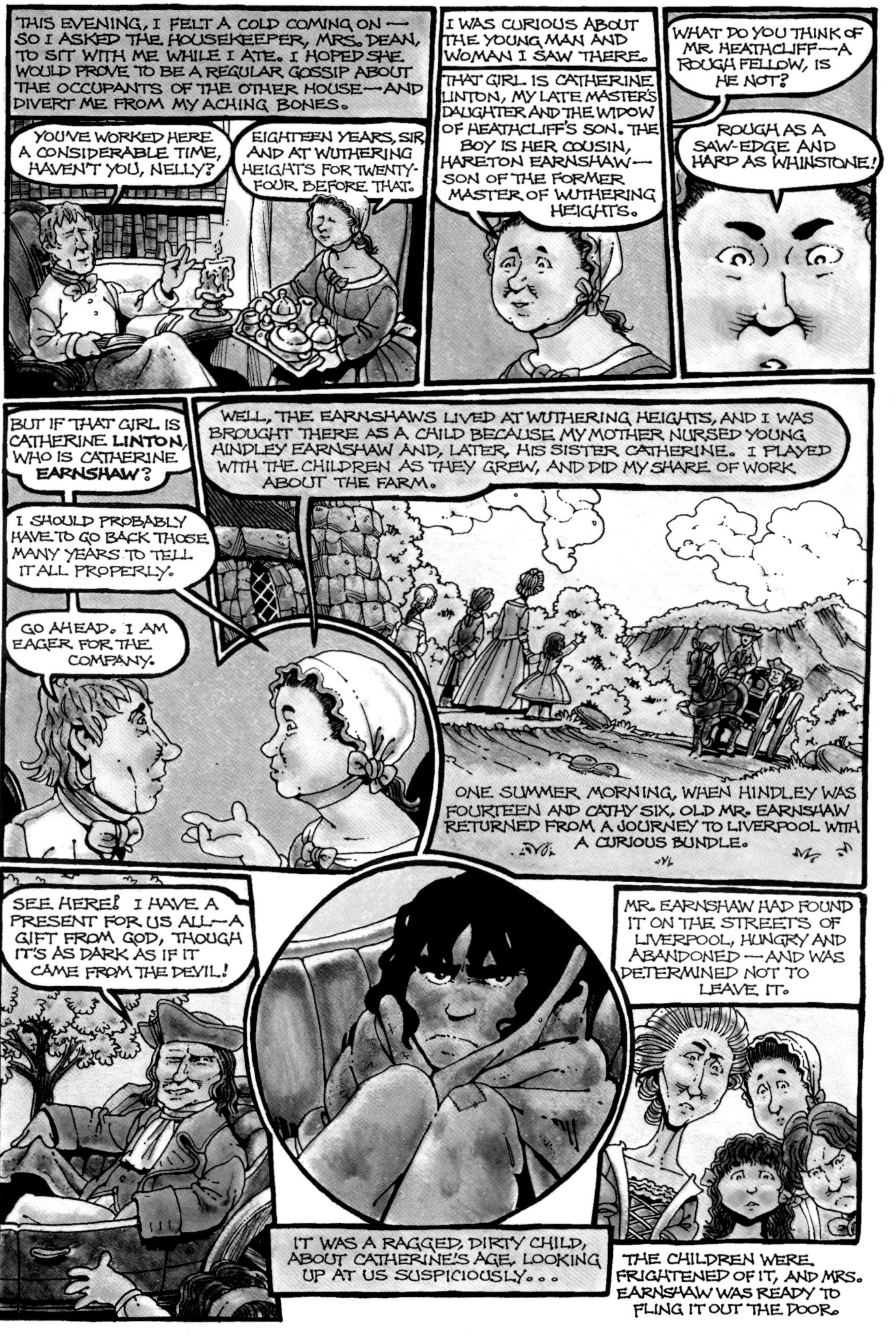
THIS EVENING, I FELT A COLD COMING ON — SO I ASKED THE HOUSEKEEPER, MRS. DEAN, TO SIT WITH ME WHILE I ATE. I HOPED SHE WOULD PROVE TO BE A REGULAR GOSSIP ABOUT THE OCCUPANTS OF THE OTHER HOUSE — AND DIVERT ME FROM MY ACHING BONES.
YOU'VE WORKED HERE A CONSIDERABLE TIME, HAVEN'T YOU, NELLY?
EIGHTEEN YEARS, SIR, AND AT WUTHERING HEIGHTS FOR TWENTY-FOUR BEFORE THAT.
I WAS CURIOUS ABOUT THE YOUNG MAN AND WOMAN I SAW THERE.
THAT GIRL IS CATHERINE LINTON, MY LATE MASTER'S DAUGHTER AND THE WIDOW OF HEATHCLIFF'S SON. THE BOY IS HER COUSIN, HARETON EARNSHAW — SON OF THE FORMER MASTER OF WUTHERING HEIGHTS.
WHAT DO YOU THINK OF MR. HEATHCLIFF — A ROUGH FELLOW, IS HE NOT?
ROUGH AS A SAW-EDGE AND HARD AS WHINSTONE!
BUT IF THAT GIRL IS CATHERINE **LINTON**, WHO IS CATHERINE **EARNSHAW**?
I SHOULD PROBABLY HAVE TO GO BACK THOSE MANY YEARS TO TELL IT ALL PROPERLY.
GO AHEAD. I AM EAGER FOR THE COMPANY.
WELL, THE EARNSHAWS LIVED AT WUTHERING HEIGHTS, AND I WAS BROUGHT THERE AS A CHILD BECAUSE MY MOTHER NURSED YOUNG HINDLEY EARNSHAW AND, LATER, HIS SISTER CATHERINE. I PLAYED WITH THE CHILDREN AS THEY GREW, AND DID MY SHARE OF WORK ABOUT THE FARM.
ONE SUMMER MORNING, WHEN HINDLEY WAS FOURTEEN AND CATHY SIX, OLD MR. EARNSHAW RETURNED FROM A JOURNEY TO LIVERPOOL WITH A CURIOUS BUNDLE.
SEE HERE! I HAVE A PRESENT FOR US ALL — A GIFT FROM GOD, THOUGH IT'S AS DARK AS IF IT CAME FROM THE DEVIL!
IT WAS A RAGGED, DIRTY CHILD, ABOUT CATHERINE'S AGE, LOOKING UP AT US SUSPICIOUSLY...
MR. EARNSHAW HAD FOUND IT ON THE STREETS OF LIVERPOOL, HUNGRY AND ABANDONED — AND WAS DETERMINED NOT TO LEAVE IT.
THE CHILDREN WERE FRIGHTENED OF IT, AND MRS. EARNSHAW WAS READY TO FLING IT OUT THE DOOR.

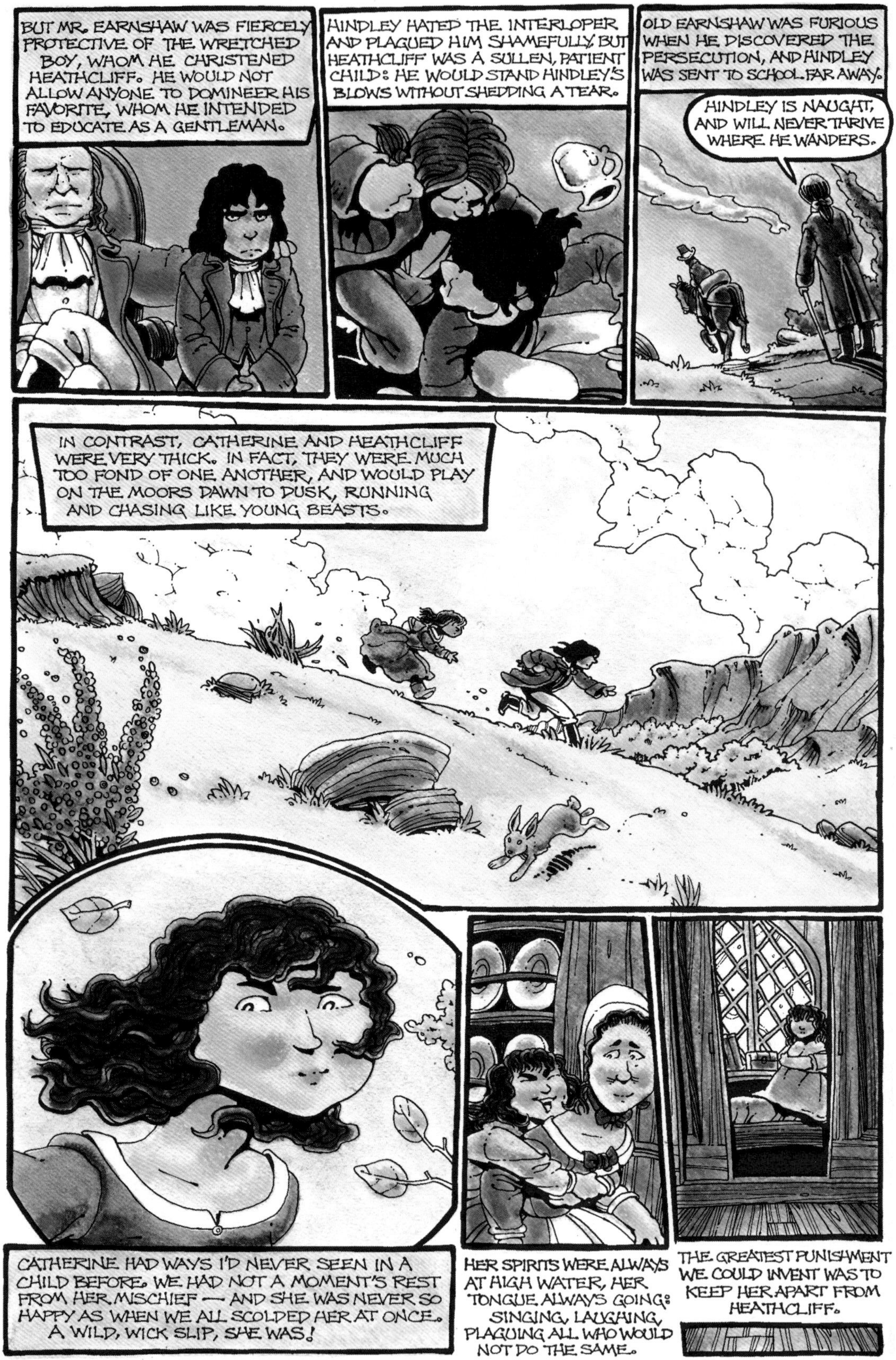
BUT MR. EARNSHAW WAS FIERCELY PROTECTIVE OF THE WRETCHED BOY, WHOM HE CHRISTENED HEATHCLIFF. HE WOULD NOT ALLOW ANYONE TO DOMINEER HIS FAVORITE, WHOM HE INTENDED TO EDUCATE AS A GENTLEMAN.
HINDLEY HATED THE INTERLOPER AND PLAGUED HIM SHAMEFULLY, BUT HEATHCLIFF WAS A SULLEN, PATIENT CHILD: HE WOULD STAND HINDLEY'S BLOWS WITHOUT SHEDDING A TEAR.
OLD EARNSHAW WAS FURIOUS WHEN HE DISCOVERED THE PERSECUTION, AND HINDLEY WAS SENT TO SCHOOL FAR AWAY.
HINDLEY IS NAUGHT, AND WILL NEVER THRIVE WHERE HE WANDERS.
IN CONTRAST, CATHERINE AND HEATHCLIFF WERE VERY THICK. IN FACT, THEY WERE MUCH TOO FOND OF ONE ANOTHER, AND WOULD PLAY ON THE MOORS DAWN TO DUSK, RUNNING AND CHASING LIKE YOUNG BEASTS.
CATHERINE HAD WAYS I'D NEVER SEEN IN A CHILD BEFORE. WE HAD NOT A MOMENT'S REST FROM HER MISCHIEF — AND SHE WAS NEVER SO HAPPY AS WHEN WE ALL SCOLDED HER AT ONCE. A WILD, WICK SLIP, SHE WAS!
HER SPIRITS WERE ALWAYS AT HIGH WATER, HER TONGUE ALWAYS GOING: SINGING, LAUGHING, PLAGUING ALL WHO WOULD NOT DO THE SAME.
THE GREATEST PUNISHMENT WE COULD INVENT WAS TO KEEP HER APART FROM HEATHCLIFF.

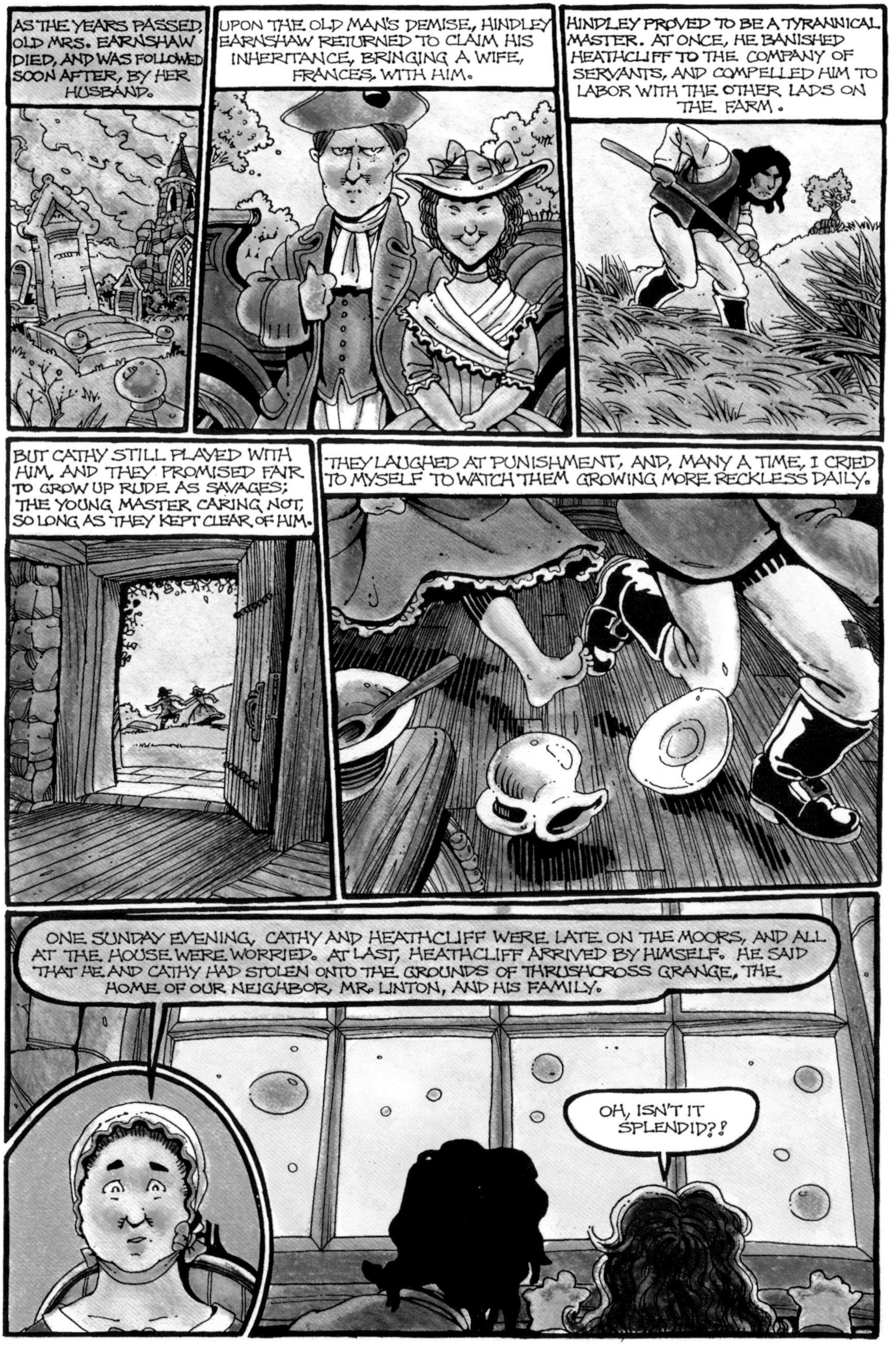
AS THE YEARS PASSED, OLD MRS. EARNSHAW DIED, AND WAS FOLLOWED SOON AFTER, BY HER HUSBAND.
UPON THE OLD MAN'S DEMISE, HINDLEY EARNSHAW RETURNED TO CLAIM HIS INHERITANCE, BRINGING A WIFE, FRANCES, WITH HIM.
HINDLEY PROVED TO BE A TYRANNICAL MASTER. AT ONCE, HE BANISHED HEATHCLIFF TO THE COMPANY OF SERVANTS, AND COMPELLED HIM TO LABOR WITH THE OTHER LADS ON THE FARM.
BUT CATHY STILL PLAYED WITH HIM, AND THEY PROMISED FAIR TO GROW UP RUDE AS SAVAGES; THE YOUNG MASTER CARING NOT, SO LONG AS THEY KEPT CLEAR OF HIM.
THEY LAUGHED AT PUNISHMENT, AND, MANY A TIME, I CRIED TO MYSELF TO WATCH THEM GROWING MORE RECKLESS DAILY.
ONE SUNDAY EVENING, CATHY AND HEATHCLIFF WERE LATE ON THE MOORS, AND ALL AT THE HOUSE WERE WORRIED. AT LAST, HEATHCLIFF ARRIVED BY HIMSELF. HE SAID THAT HE AND CATHY HAD STOLEN ONTO THE GROUNDS OF THRUSHCROSS GRANGE, THE HOME OF OUR NEIGHBOR, MR. LINTON, AND HIS FAMILY.
OH, ISN'T IT SPLENDID?!

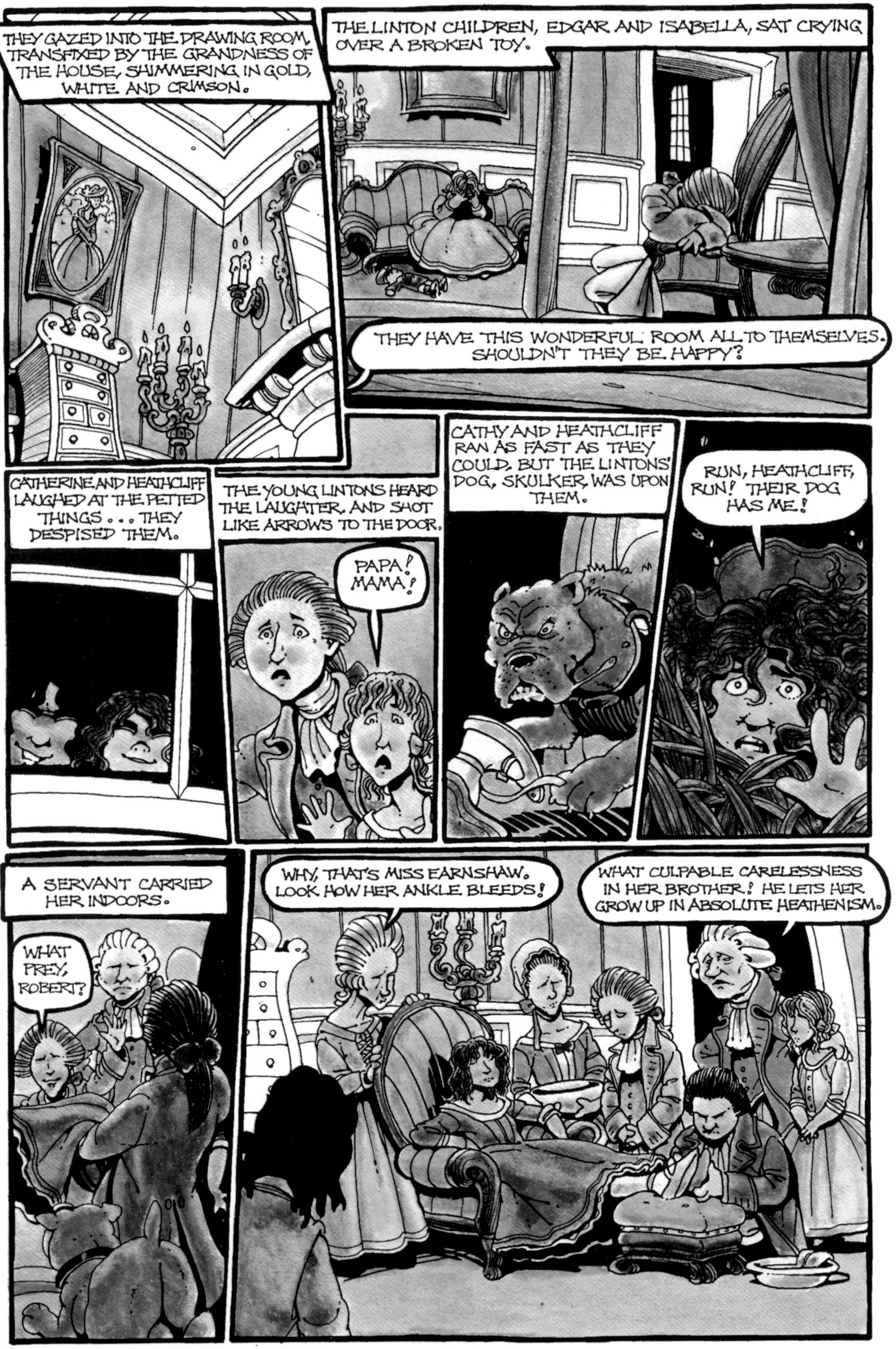
THEY GAZED INTO THE DRAWING ROOM, TRANSFIXED BY THE GRANDNESS OF THE HOUSE, SHIMMERING IN GOLD, WHITE AND CRIMSON.
THE LINTON CHILDREN, EDGAR AND ISABELLA, SAT CRYING OVER A BROKEN TOY.
THEY HAVE THIS WONDERFUL ROOM ALL TO THEMSELVES. SHOULDN'T THEY BE HAPPY?
CATHERINE AND HEATHCLIFF LAUGHED AT THE PETTED THINGS . . . THEY DESPISED THEM.
THE YOUNG LINTONS HEARD THE LAUGHTER, AND SHOT LIKE ARROWS TO THE DOOR.
PAPA! MAMA!
CATHY AND HEATHCLIFF RAN AS FAST AS THEY COULD, BUT THE LINTONS' DOG, SKULKER, WAS UPON THEM.
RUN, HEATHCLIFF, RUN! THEIR DOG HAS ME!
A SERVANT CARRIED HER INDOORS.
WHAT PREY, ROBERT?
WHY, THAT'S MISS EARNSHAW. LOOK HOW HER ANKLE BLEEDS!
WHAT CULPABLE CARELESSNESS IN HER BROTHER! HE LETS HER GROW UP IN ABSOLUTE HEATHENISM.

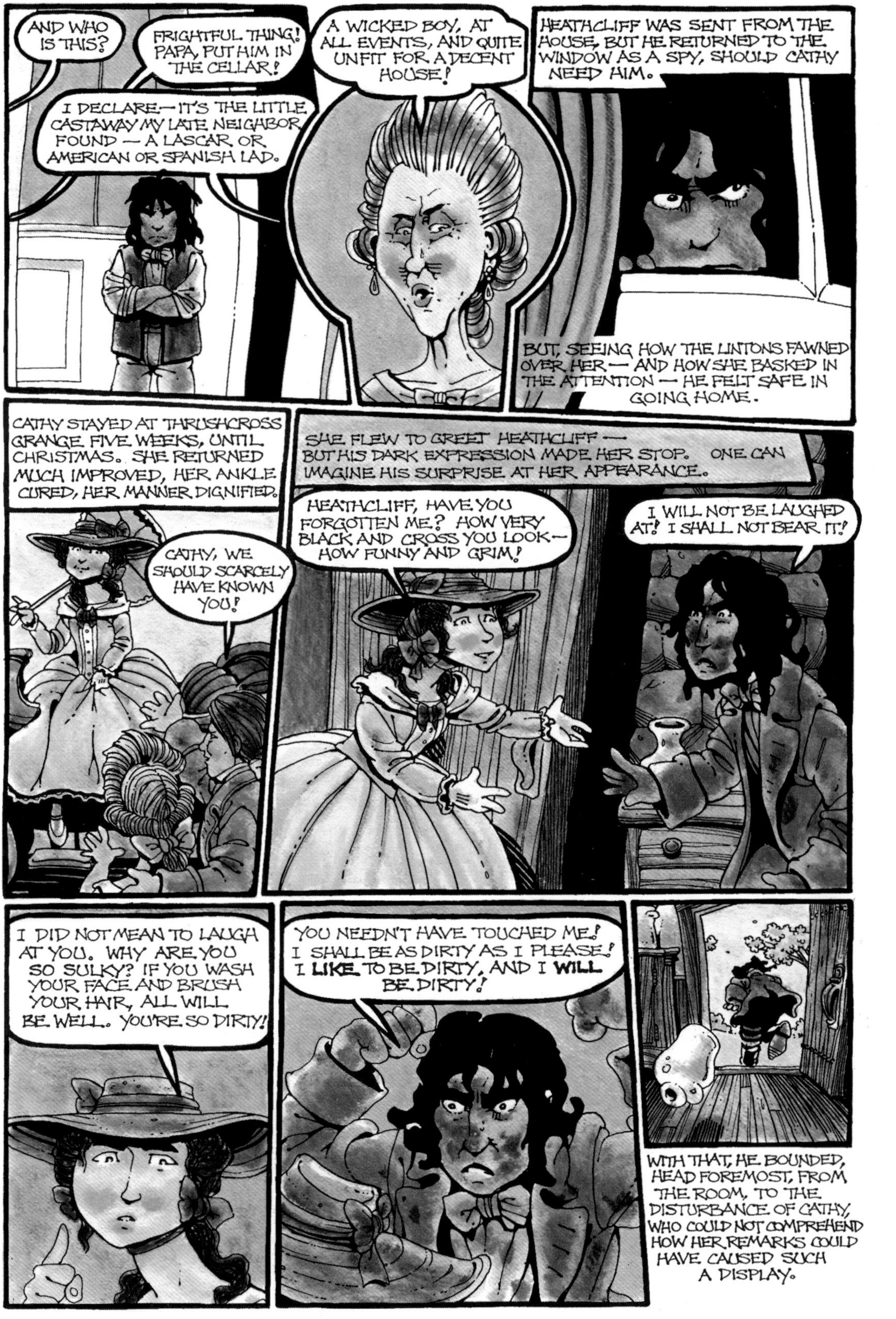
AND WHO IS THIS?
FRIGHTFUL THING! PAPA, PUT HIM IN THE CELLAR!
I DECLARE— IT'S THE LITTLE CASTAWAY MY LATE NEIGHBOR FOUND — A LASCAR OR AMERICAN OR SPANISH LAD.
A WICKED BOY, AT ALL EVENTS, AND QUITE UNFIT FOR A DECENT HOUSE!
HEATHCLIFF WAS SENT FROM THE HOUSE, BUT HE RETURNED TO THE WINDOW AS A SPY, SHOULD CATHY NEED HIM.
BUT, SEEING HOW THE LINTONS FAWNED OVER HER — AND HOW SHE BASKED IN THE ATTENTION — HE FELT SAFE IN GOING HOME.
CATHY STAYED AT THRUSHCROSS GRANGE FIVE WEEKS, UNTIL CHRISTMAS. SHE RETURNED MUCH IMPROVED, HER ANKLE CURED, HER MANNER DIGNIFIED.
CATHY, WE SHOULD SCARCELY HAVE KNOWN YOU!
SHE FLEW TO GREET HEATHCLIFF — BUT HIS DARK EXPRESSION MADE HER STOP. ONE CAN IMAGINE HIS SURPRISE AT HER APPEARANCE.
HEATHCLIFF, HAVE YOU FORGOTTEN ME? HOW VERY BLACK AND CROSS YOU LOOK— HOW FUNNY AND GRIM!
I WILL NOT BE LAUGHED AT! I SHALL NOT BEAR IT!
I DID NOT MEAN TO LAUGH AT YOU. WHY ARE YOU SO SULKY? IF YOU WASH YOUR FACE AND BRUSH YOUR HAIR, ALL WILL BE WELL. YOU'RE SO DIRTY!
YOU NEEDN'T HAVE TOUCHED ME! I SHALL BE AS DIRTY AS I PLEASE! I **LIKE** TO BE DIRTY, AND I **WILL** BE DIRTY!
WITH THAT, HE BOUNDED, HEAD FOREMOST, FROM THE ROOM, TO THE DISTURBANCE OF CATHY, WHO COULD NOT COMPREHEND HOW HER REMARKS COULD HAVE CAUSED SUCH A DISPLAY.

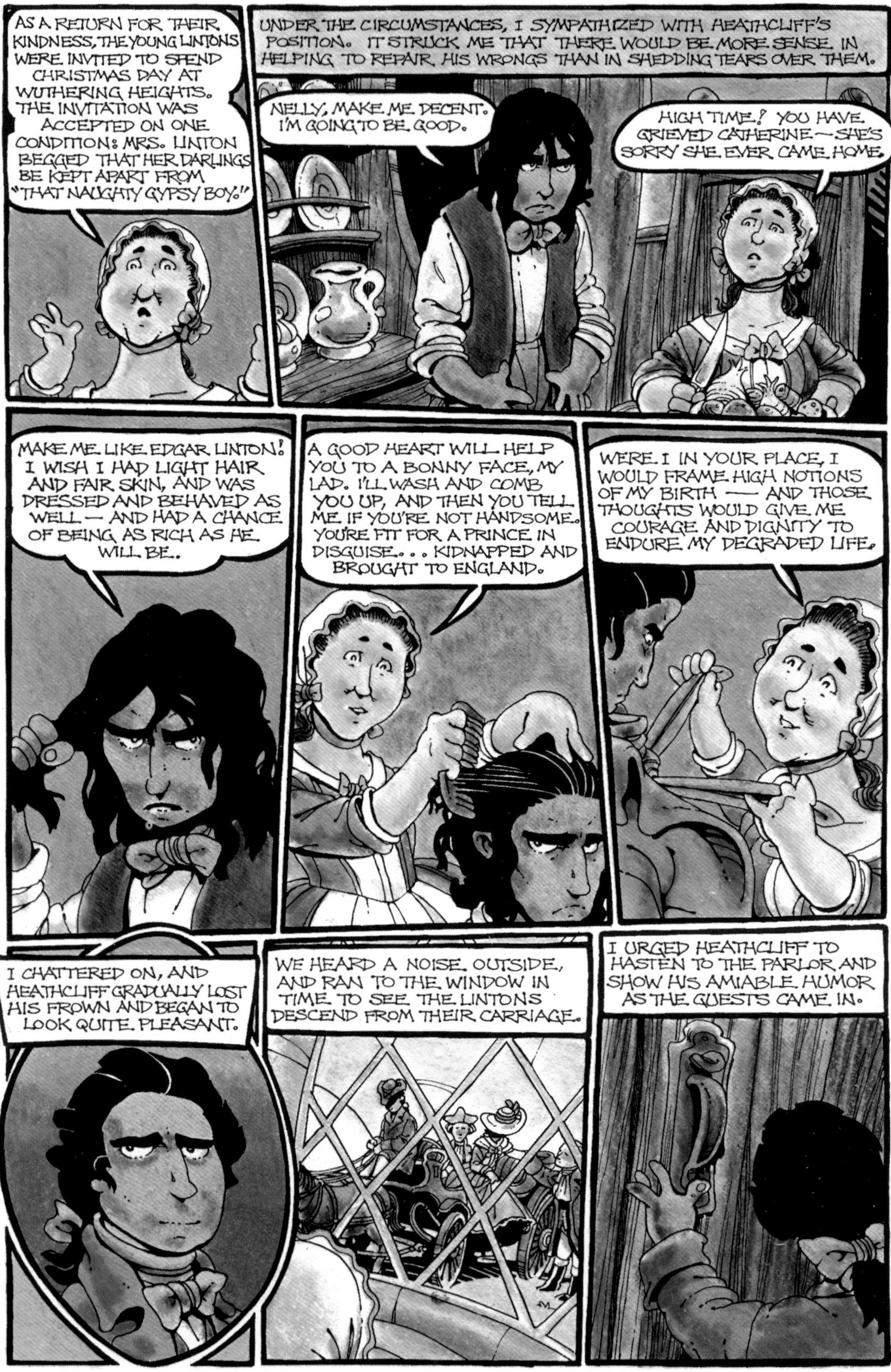
AS A RETURN FOR THEIR KINDNESS, THE YOUNG LINTONS WERE INVITED TO SPEND CHRISTMAS DAY AT WUTHERING HEIGHTS. THE INVITATION WAS ACCEPTED ON ONE CONDITION: MRS. LINTON BEGGED THAT HER DARLINGS BE KEPT APART FROM "THAT NAUGHTY GYPSY BOY."
UNDER THE CIRCUMSTANCES, I SYMPATHIZED WITH HEATHCLIFF'S POSITION. IT STRUCK ME THAT THERE WOULD BE MORE SENSE IN HELPING TO REPAIR HIS WRONGS THAN IN SHEDDING TEARS OVER THEM.
NELLY, MAKE ME DECENT. I'M GOING TO BE GOOD.
HIGH TIME! YOU HAVE GRIEVED CATHERINE — SHE'S SORRY SHE EVER CAME HOME.
MAKE ME LIKE EDGAR LINTON! I WISH I HAD LIGHT HAIR AND FAIR SKIN, AND WAS DRESSED AND BEHAVED AS WELL — AND HAD A CHANCE OF BEING AS RICH AS HE WILL BE.
A GOOD HEART WILL HELP YOU TO A BONNY FACE, MY LAD. I'LL WASH AND COMB YOU UP, AND THEN YOU TELL ME IF YOU'RE NOT HANDSOME. YOU'RE FIT FOR A PRINCE IN DISGUISE... KIDNAPPED AND BROUGHT TO ENGLAND.
WERE I IN YOUR PLACE, I WOULD FRAME HIGH NOTIONS OF MY BIRTH — AND THOSE THOUGHTS WOULD GIVE ME COURAGE AND DIGNITY TO ENDURE MY DEGRADED LIFE.
I CHATTERED ON, AND HEATHCLIFF GRADUALLY LOST HIS FROWN AND BEGAN TO LOOK QUITE PLEASANT.
WE HEARD A NOISE OUTSIDE, AND RAN TO THE WINDOW IN TIME TO SEE THE LINTONS DESCEND FROM THEIR CARRIAGE.
I URGED HEATHCLIFF TO HASTEN TO THE PARLOR AND SHOW HIS AMIABLE HUMOR AS THE GUESTS CAME IN.

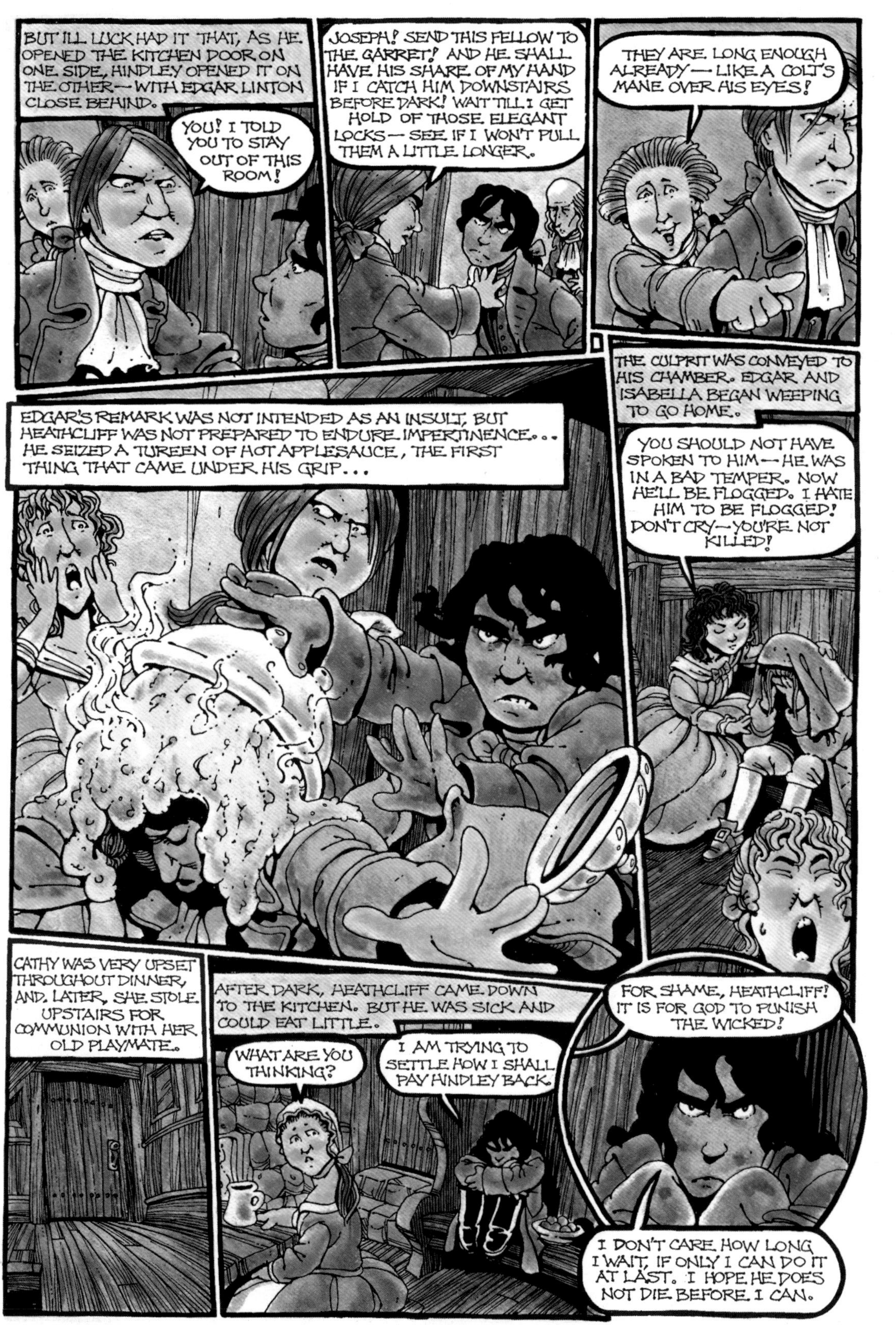

BUT ILL LUCK HAD IT THAT, AS HE OPENED THE KITCHEN DOOR ON ONE SIDE, HINDLEY OPENED IT ON THE OTHER— WITH EDGAR LINTON CLOSE BEHIND.
YOU! I TOLD YOU TO STAY OUT OF THIS ROOM!
JOSEPH! SEND THIS FELLOW TO THE GARRET! AND HE SHALL HAVE HIS SHARE OF MY HAND IF I CATCH HIM DOWNSTAIRS BEFORE DARK! WAIT TILL I GET HOLD OF THOSE ELEGANT LOCKS— SEE IF I WON'T PULL THEM A LITTLE LONGER.
THEY ARE LONG ENOUGH ALREADY— LIKE A COLT'S MANE OVER HIS EYES!
EDGAR'S REMARK WAS NOT INTENDED AS AN INSULT, BUT HEATHCLIFF WAS NOT PREPARED TO ENDURE IMPERTINENCE... HE SEIZED A TUREEN OF HOT APPLESAUCE, THE FIRST THING THAT CAME UNDER HIS GRIP...
THE CULPRIT WAS CONVEYED TO HIS CHAMBER. EDGAR AND ISABELLA BEGAN WEEPING TO GO HOME.
YOU SHOULD NOT HAVE SPOKEN TO HIM— HE WAS IN A BAD TEMPER. NOW HE'LL BE FLOGGED. I HATE HIM TO BE FLOGGED! DON'T CRY— YOU'RE NOT KILLED!
CATHY WAS VERY UPSET THROUGHOUT DINNER, AND, LATER, SHE STOLE UPSTAIRS FOR COMMUNION WITH HER OLD PLAYMATE.
AFTER DARK, HEATHCLIFF CAME DOWN TO THE KITCHEN. BUT HE WAS SICK AND COULD EAT LITTLE.
WHAT ARE YOU THINKING?
I AM TRYING TO SETTLE HOW I SHALL PAY HINDLEY BACK.
FOR SHAME, HEATHCLIFF! IT IS FOR GOD TO PUNISH THE WICKED!
I DON'T CARE HOW LONG I WAIT, IF ONLY I CAN DO IT AT LAST. I HOPE HE DOES NOT DIE BEFORE I CAN.

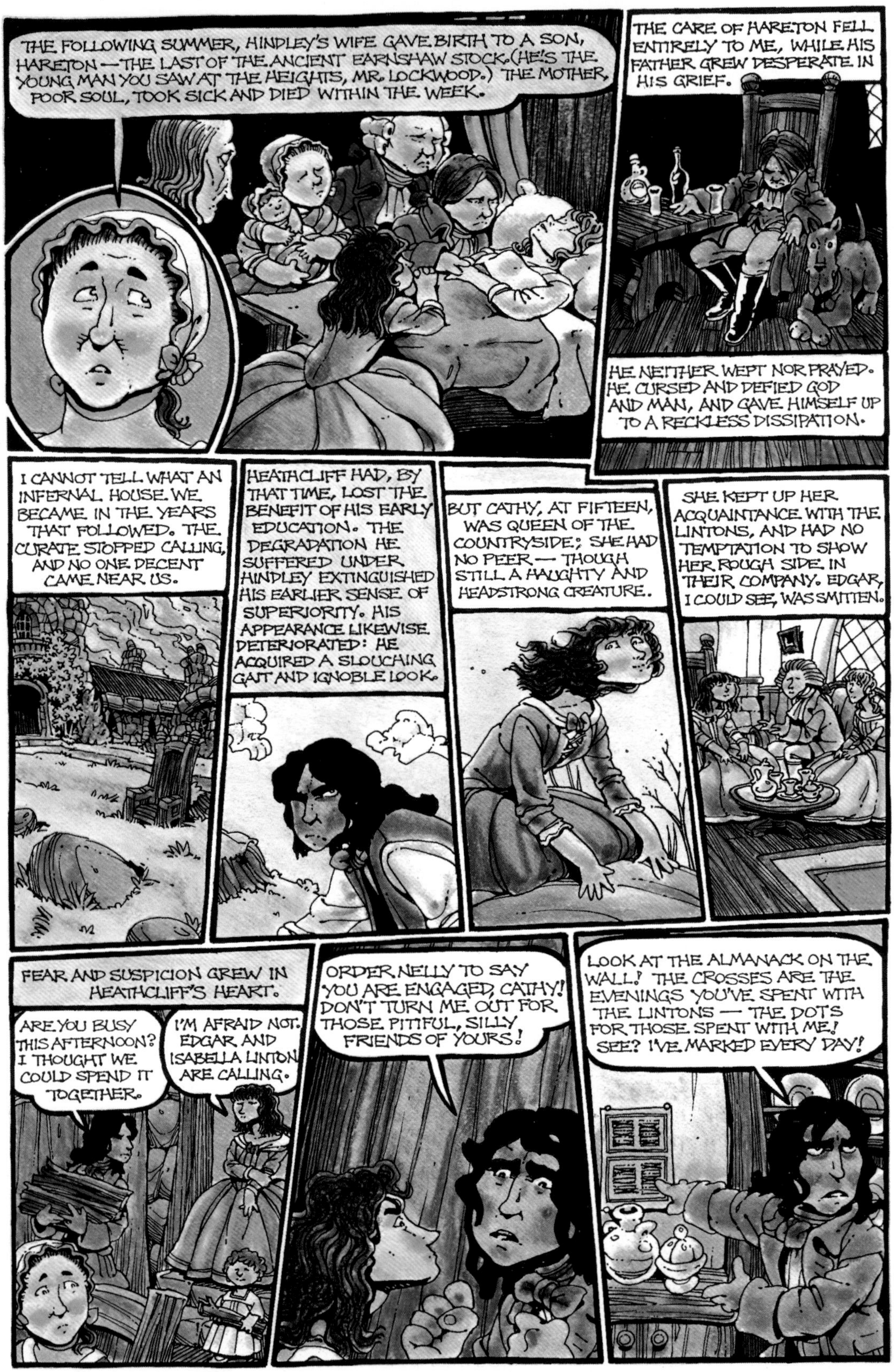

THE FOLLOWING SUMMER, HINDLEY'S WIFE GAVE BIRTH TO A SON, HARETON — THE LAST OF THE ANCIENT EARNSHAW STOCK. (HE'S THE YOUNG MAN YOU SAW AT THE HEIGHTS, MR. LOCKWOOD.) THE MOTHER, POOR SOUL, TOOK SICK AND DIED WITHIN THE WEEK.
THE CARE OF HARETON FELL ENTIRELY TO ME, WHILE HIS FATHER GREW DESPERATE IN HIS GRIEF.
HE NEITHER WEPT NOR PRAYED. HE CURSED AND DEFIED GOD AND MAN, AND GAVE HIMSELF UP TO A RECKLESS DISSIPATION.
I CANNOT TELL WHAT AN INFERNAL HOUSE WE BECAME IN THE YEARS THAT FOLLOWED. THE CURATE STOPPED CALLING, AND NO ONE DECENT CAME NEAR US.
HEATHCLIFF HAD, BY THAT TIME, LOST THE BENEFIT OF HIS EARLY EDUCATION. THE DEGRADATION HE SUFFERED UNDER HINDLEY EXTINGUISHED HIS EARLIER SENSE OF SUPERIORITY. HIS APPEARANCE LIKEWISE DETERIORATED: HE ACQUIRED A SLOUCHING GAIT AND IGNOBLE LOOK.
BUT CATHY, AT FIFTEEN, WAS QUEEN OF THE COUNTRYSIDE; SHE HAD NO PEER — THOUGH STILL A HAUGHTY AND HEADSTRONG CREATURE.
SHE KEPT UP HER ACQUAINTANCE WITH THE LINTONS, AND HAD NO TEMPTATION TO SHOW HER ROUGH SIDE IN THEIR COMPANY. EDGAR, I COULD SEE, WAS SMITTEN.
FEAR AND SUSPICION GREW IN HEATHCLIFF'S HEART.
ARE YOU BUSY THIS AFTERNOON? I THOUGHT WE COULD SPEND IT TOGETHER.
I'M AFRAID NOT. EDGAR AND ISABELLA LINTON ARE CALLING.
ORDER NELLY TO SAY YOU ARE ENGAGED, CATHY! DON'T TURN ME OUT FOR THOSE PITIFUL, SILLY FRIENDS OF YOURS!
LOOK AT THE ALMANACK ON THE WALL! THE CROSSES ARE THE EVENINGS YOU'VE SPENT WITH THE LINTONS — THE DOTS FOR THOSE SPENT WITH ME! SEE? I'VE MARKED EVERY DAY!

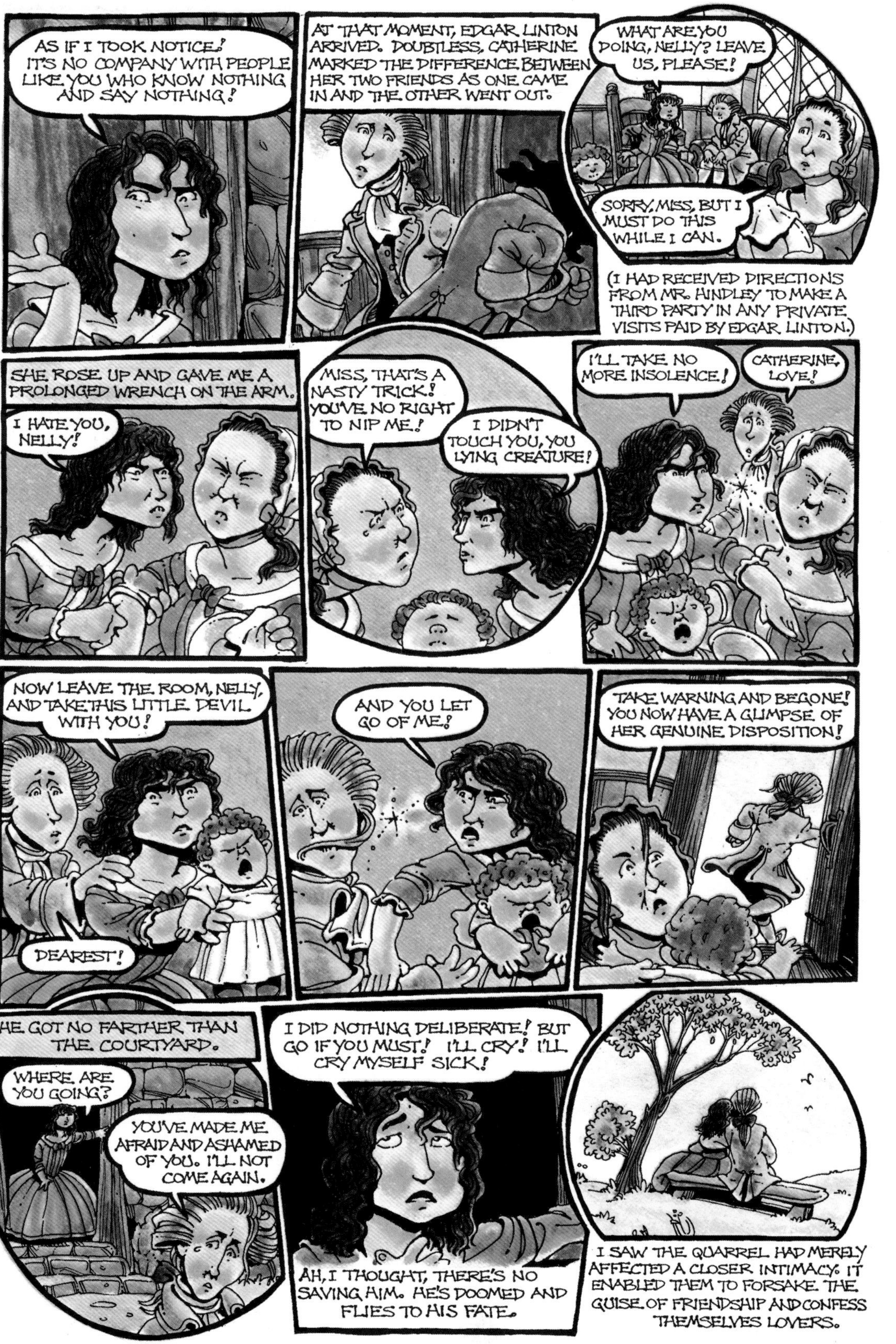
AS IF I TOOK NOTICE! IT'S NO COMPANY WITH PEOPLE LIKE YOU WHO KNOW NOTHING AND SAY NOTHING!
AT THAT MOMENT, EDGAR LINTON ARRIVED. DOUBTLESS, CATHERINE MARKED THE DIFFERENCE BETWEEN HER TWO FRIENDS AS ONE CAME IN AND THE OTHER WENT OUT.
WHAT ARE YOU DOING, NELLY? LEAVE US, PLEASE!
SORRY, MISS, BUT I MUST DO THIS WHILE I CAN.
(I HAD RECEIVED DIRECTIONS FROM MR. HINDLEY TO MAKE A THIRD PARTY IN ANY PRIVATE VISITS PAID BY EDGAR LINTON.)
SHE ROSE UP AND GAVE ME A PROLONGED WRENCH ON THE ARM.
I HATE YOU, NELLY!
MISS, THAT'S A NASTY TRICK! YOU'VE NO RIGHT TO NIP ME!
I DIDN'T TOUCH YOU, YOU LYING CREATURE!
I'LL TAKE NO MORE INSOLENCE!
CATHERINE, LOVE!
NOW LEAVE THE ROOM, NELLY, AND TAKE THIS LITTLE DEVIL WITH YOU!
DEAREST!
AND YOU LET GO OF ME!
TAKE WARNING AND BEGONE! YOU NOW HAVE A GLIMPSE OF HER GENUINE DISPOSITION!
HE GOT NO FARTHER THAN THE COURTYARD.
WHERE ARE YOU GOING?
YOU'VE MADE ME AFRAID AND ASHAMED OF YOU. I'LL NOT COME AGAIN.
I DID NOTHING DELIBERATE! BUT GO IF YOU MUST! I'LL CRY! I'LL CRY MYSELF SICK!
AH, I THOUGHT, THERE'S NO SAVING HIM. HE'S DOOMED AND FLIES TO HIS FATE.
I SAW THE QUARREL HAD MERELY AFFECTED A CLOSER INTIMACY. IT ENABLED THEM TO FORSAKE THE GUISE OF FRIENDSHIP AND CONFESS THEMSELVES LOVERS.

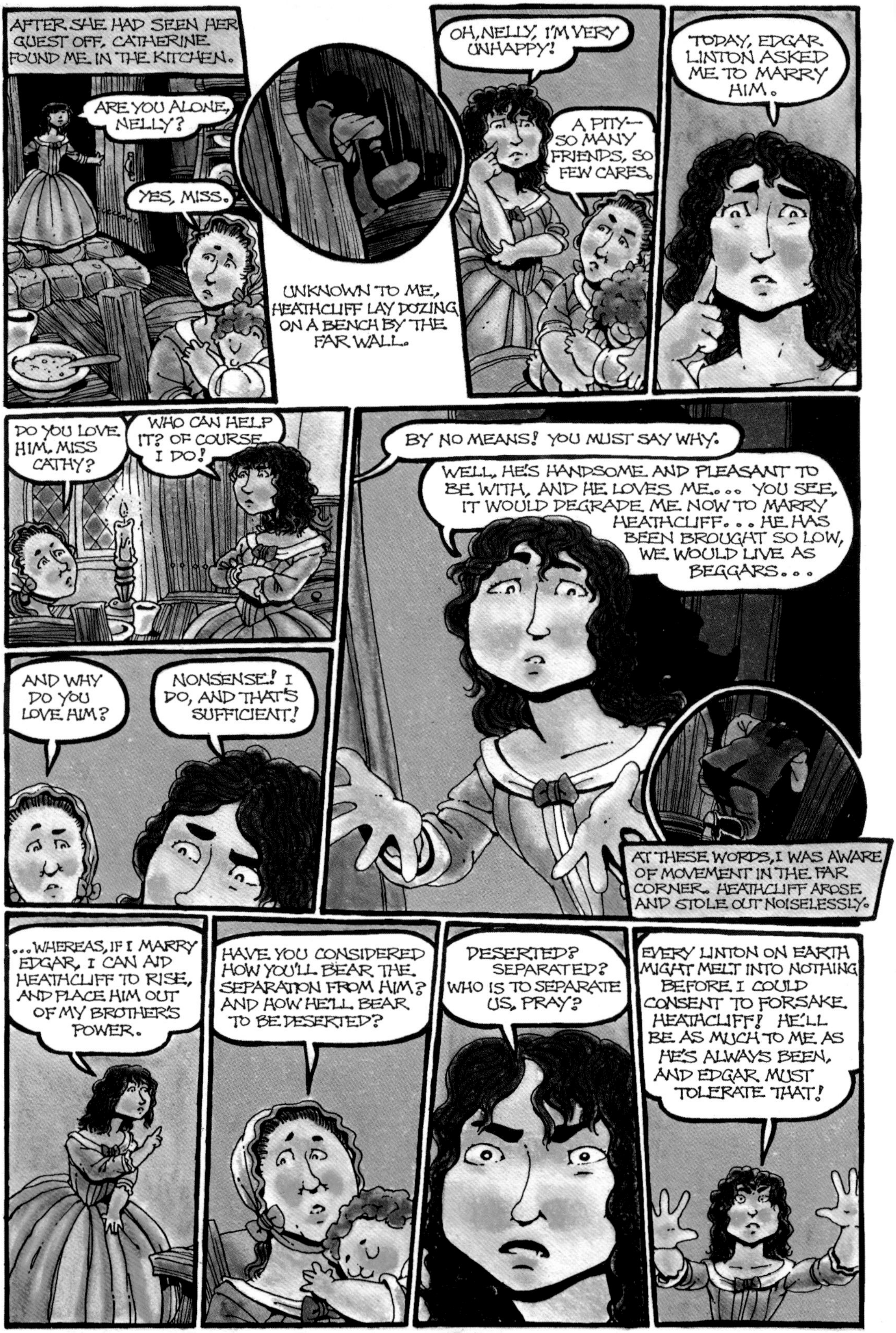
AFTER SHE HAD SEEN HER GUEST OFF, CATHERINE FOUND ME IN THE KITCHEN.
ARE YOU ALONE, NELLY?
YES, MISS.
UNKNOWN TO ME, HEATHCLIFF LAY DOZING ON A BENCH BY THE FAR WALL.
OH, NELLY, I'M VERY UNHAPPY!
A PITY— SO MANY FRIENDS, SO FEW CARES.
TODAY, EDGAR LINTON ASKED ME TO MARRY HIM.
DO YOU LOVE HIM, MISS CATHY?
WHO CAN HELP IT? OF COURSE I DO!
AND WHY DO YOU LOVE HIM?
NONSENSE! I DO, AND THAT'S SUFFICIENT!
BY NO MEANS! YOU MUST SAY WHY.
WELL, HE'S HANDSOME AND PLEASANT TO BE WITH, AND HE LOVES ME... YOU SEE, IT WOULD DEGRADE ME NOW TO MARRY HEATHCLIFF... HE HAS BEEN BROUGHT SO LOW, WE WOULD LIVE AS BEGGARS...
AT THESE WORDS, I WAS AWARE OF MOVEMENT IN THE FAR CORNER. HEATHCLIFF AROSE AND STOLE OUT NOISELESSLY.
...WHEREAS, IF I MARRY EDGAR, I CAN AID HEATHCLIFF TO RISE, AND PLACE HIM OUT OF MY BROTHER'S POWER.
HAVE YOU CONSIDERED HOW YOU'LL BEAR THE SEPARATION FROM HIM? AND HOW HE'LL BEAR TO BE DESERTED?
DESERTED? SEPARATED? WHO IS TO SEPARATE US, PRAY?
EVERY LINTON ON EARTH MIGHT MELT INTO NOTHING BEFORE I COULD CONSENT TO FORSAKE HEATHCLIFF! HE'LL BE AS MUCH TO ME AS HE'S ALWAYS BEEN, AND EDGAR MUST TOLERATE THAT!

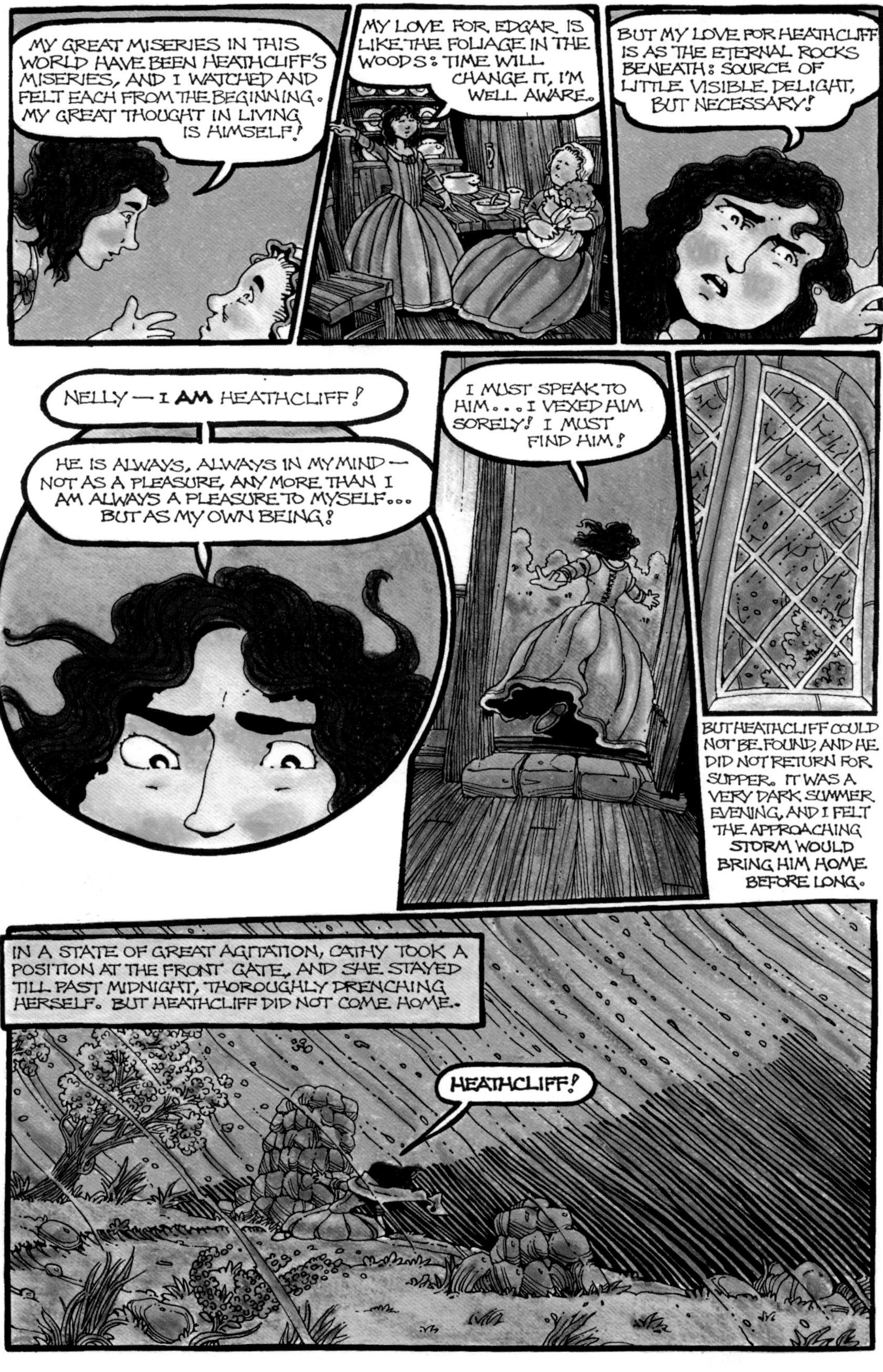
MY GREAT MISERIES IN THIS WORLD HAVE BEEN HEATHCLIFF'S MISERIES, AND I WATCHED AND FELT EACH FROM THE BEGINNING. MY GREAT THOUGHT IN LIVING IS HIMSELF!
MY LOVE FOR EDGAR IS LIKE THE FOLIAGE IN THE WOODS: TIME WILL CHANGE IT, I'M WELL AWARE.
BUT MY LOVE FOR HEATHCLIFF IS AS THE ETERNAL ROCKS BENEATH: SOURCE OF LITTLE VISIBLE DELIGHT, BUT NECESSARY!
NELLY — I **AM** HEATHCLIFF!
HE IS ALWAYS, ALWAYS IN MY MIND — NOT AS A PLEASURE, ANY MORE THAN I AM ALWAYS A PLEASURE TO MYSELF... BUT AS MY OWN BEING!
I MUST SPEAK TO HIM... I VEXED HIM SORELY! I MUST FIND HIM!
BUT HEATHCLIFF COULD NOT BE FOUND, AND HE DID NOT RETURN FOR SUPPER. IT WAS A VERY DARK SUMMER EVENING, AND I FELT THE APPROACHING STORM WOULD BRING HIM HOME BEFORE LONG.
IN A STATE OF GREAT AGITATION, CATHY TOOK A POSITION AT THE FRONT GATE, AND SHE STAYED TILL PAST MIDNIGHT, THOROUGHLY DRENCHING HERSELF. BUT HEATHCLIFF DID NOT COME HOME.
HEATHCLIFF!

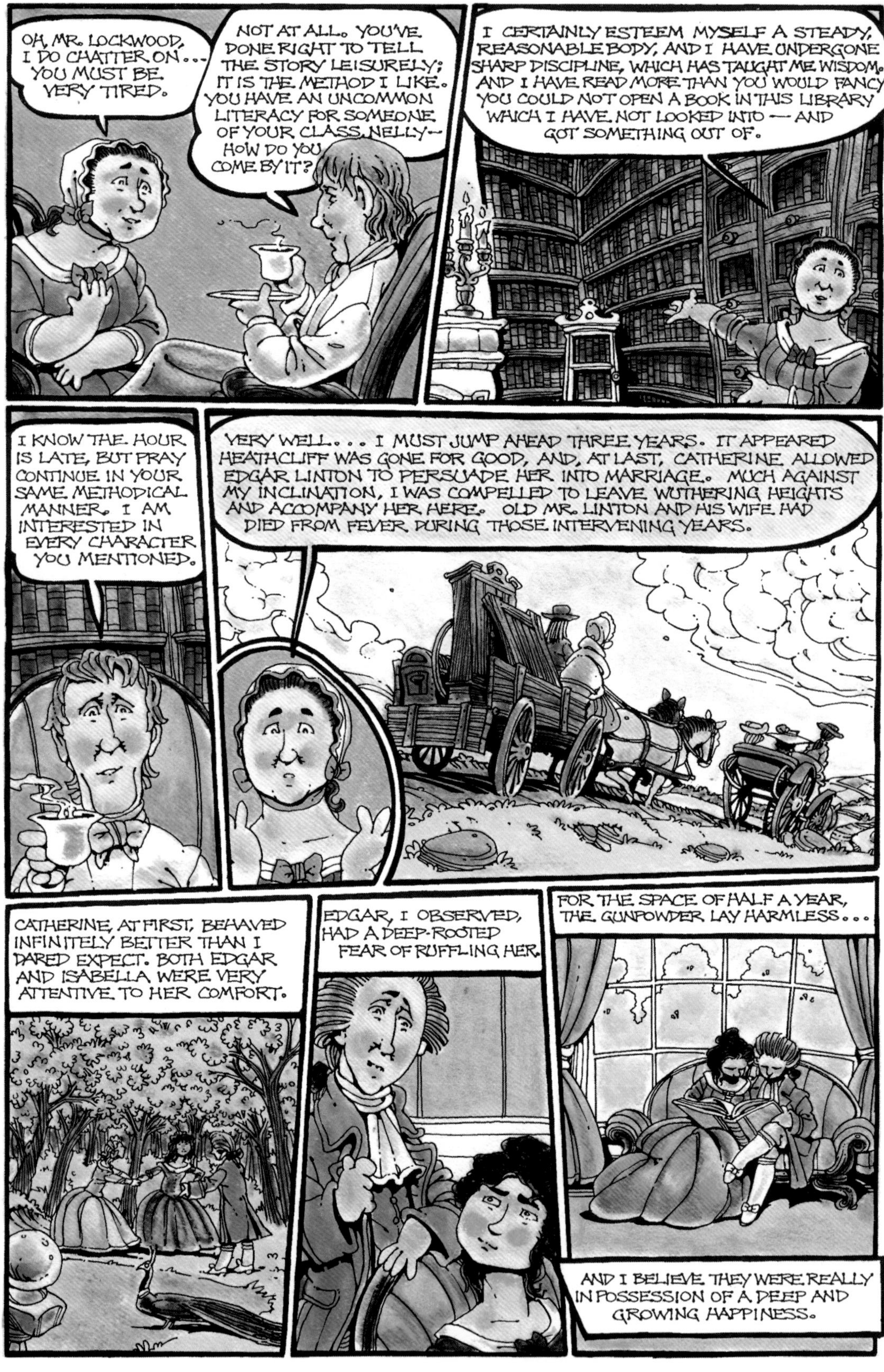
OH, MR. LOCKWOOD, I DO CHATTER ON... YOU MUST BE VERY TIRED.
NOT AT ALL. YOU'VE DONE RIGHT TO TELL THE STORY LEISURELY; IT IS THE METHOD I LIKE. YOU HAVE AN UNCOMMON LITERACY FOR SOMEONE OF YOUR CLASS, NELLY-- HOW DO YOU COME BY IT?
I CERTAINLY ESTEEM MYSELF A STEADY, REASONABLE BODY, AND I HAVE UNDERGONE SHARP DISCIPLINE, WHICH HAS TAUGHT ME WISDOM. AND I HAVE READ MORE THAN YOU WOULD FANCY: YOU COULD NOT OPEN A BOOK IN THIS LIBRARY WHICH I HAVE NOT LOOKED INTO — AND GOT SOMETHING OUT OF.
I KNOW THE HOUR IS LATE, BUT PRAY CONTINUE IN YOUR SAME METHODICAL MANNER. I AM INTERESTED IN EVERY CHARACTER YOU MENTIONED.
VERY WELL... I MUST JUMP AHEAD THREE YEARS. IT APPEARED HEATHCLIFF WAS GONE FOR GOOD, AND, AT LAST, CATHERINE ALLOWED EDGAR LINTON TO PERSUADE HER INTO MARRIAGE. MUCH AGAINST MY INCLINATION, I WAS COMPELLED TO LEAVE WUTHERING HEIGHTS AND ACCOMPANY HER HERE. OLD MR. LINTON AND HIS WIFE HAD DIED FROM FEVER DURING THOSE INTERVENING YEARS.
CATHERINE, AT FIRST, BEHAVED INFINITELY BETTER THAN I DARED EXPECT. BOTH EDGAR AND ISABELLA WERE VERY ATTENTIVE TO HER COMFORT.
EDGAR, I OBSERVED, HAD A DEEP-ROOTED FEAR OF RUFFLING HER.
FOR THE SPACE OF HALF A YEAR, THE GUNPOWDER LAY HARMLESS...
AND I BELIEVE THEY WERE REALLY IN POSSESSION OF A DEEP AND GROWING HAPPINESS.

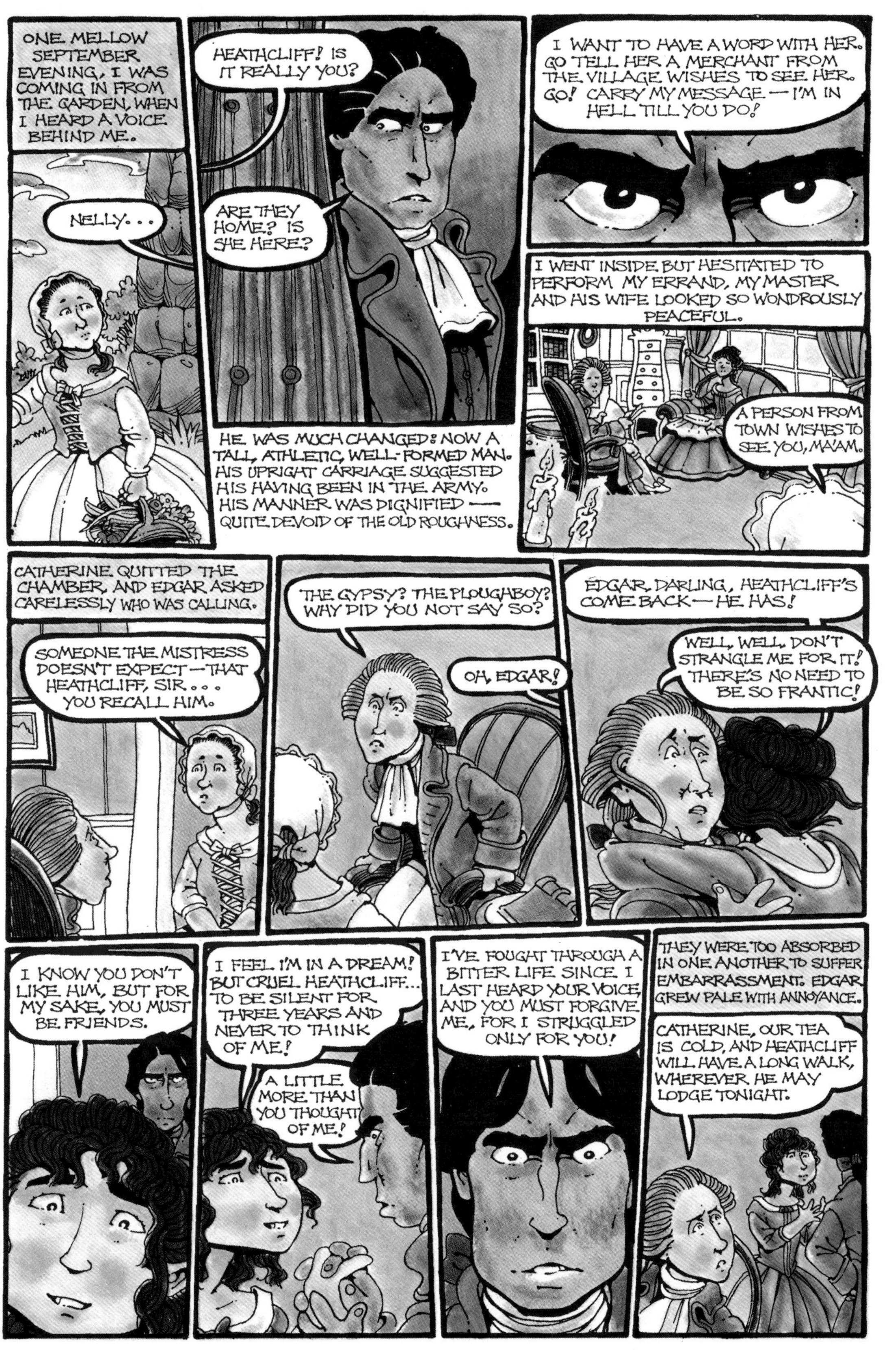
ONE MELLOW SEPTEMBER EVENING, I WAS COMING IN FROM THE GARDEN, WHEN I HEARD A VOICE BEHIND ME.
NELLY...
HEATHCLIFF! IS IT REALLY YOU?
ARE THEY HOME? IS SHE HERE?
HE WAS MUCH CHANGED: NOW A TALL, ATHLETIC, WELL-FORMED MAN. HIS UPRIGHT CARRIAGE SUGGESTED HIS HAVING BEEN IN THE ARMY. HIS MANNER WAS DIGNIFIED — QUITE DEVOID OF THE OLD ROUGHNESS.
I WANT TO HAVE A WORD WITH HER. GO TELL HER A MERCHANT FROM THE VILLAGE WISHES TO SEE HER. GO! CARRY MY MESSAGE — I'M IN HELL TILL YOU DO!
I WENT INSIDE BUT HESITATED TO PERFORM MY ERRAND, MY MASTER AND HIS WIFE LOOKED SO WONDROUSLY PEACEFUL.
A PERSON FROM TOWN WISHES TO SEE YOU, MA'AM.
CATHERINE QUITTED THE CHAMBER, AND EDGAR ASKED CARELESSLY WHO WAS CALLING.
SOMEONE THE MISTRESS DOESN'T EXPECT — THAT HEATHCLIFF, SIR... YOU RECALL HIM.
THE GYPSY? THE PLOUGHBOY? WHY DID YOU NOT SAY SO?
OH, EDGAR!
EDGAR, DARLING, HEATHCLIFF'S COME BACK — HE HAS!
WELL, WELL, DON'T STRANGLE ME FOR IT! THERE'S NO NEED TO BE SO FRANTIC!
I KNOW YOU DON'T LIKE HIM, BUT FOR MY SAKE, YOU MUST BE FRIENDS.
I FEEL I'M IN A DREAM! BUT CRUEL HEATHCLIFF... TO BE SILENT FOR THREE YEARS AND NEVER TO THINK OF ME!
A LITTLE MORE THAN YOU THOUGHT OF ME!
I'VE FOUGHT THROUGH A BITTER LIFE SINCE I LAST HEARD YOUR VOICE, AND YOU MUST FORGIVE ME, FOR I STRUGGLED ONLY FOR YOU!
THEY WERE TOO ABSORBED IN ONE ANOTHER TO SUFFER EMBARRASSMENT. EDGAR GREW PALE WITH ANNOYANCE.
CATHERINE, OUR TEA IS COLD, AND HEATHCLIFF WILL HAVE A LONG WALK, WHEREVER HE MAY LODGE TONIGHT.

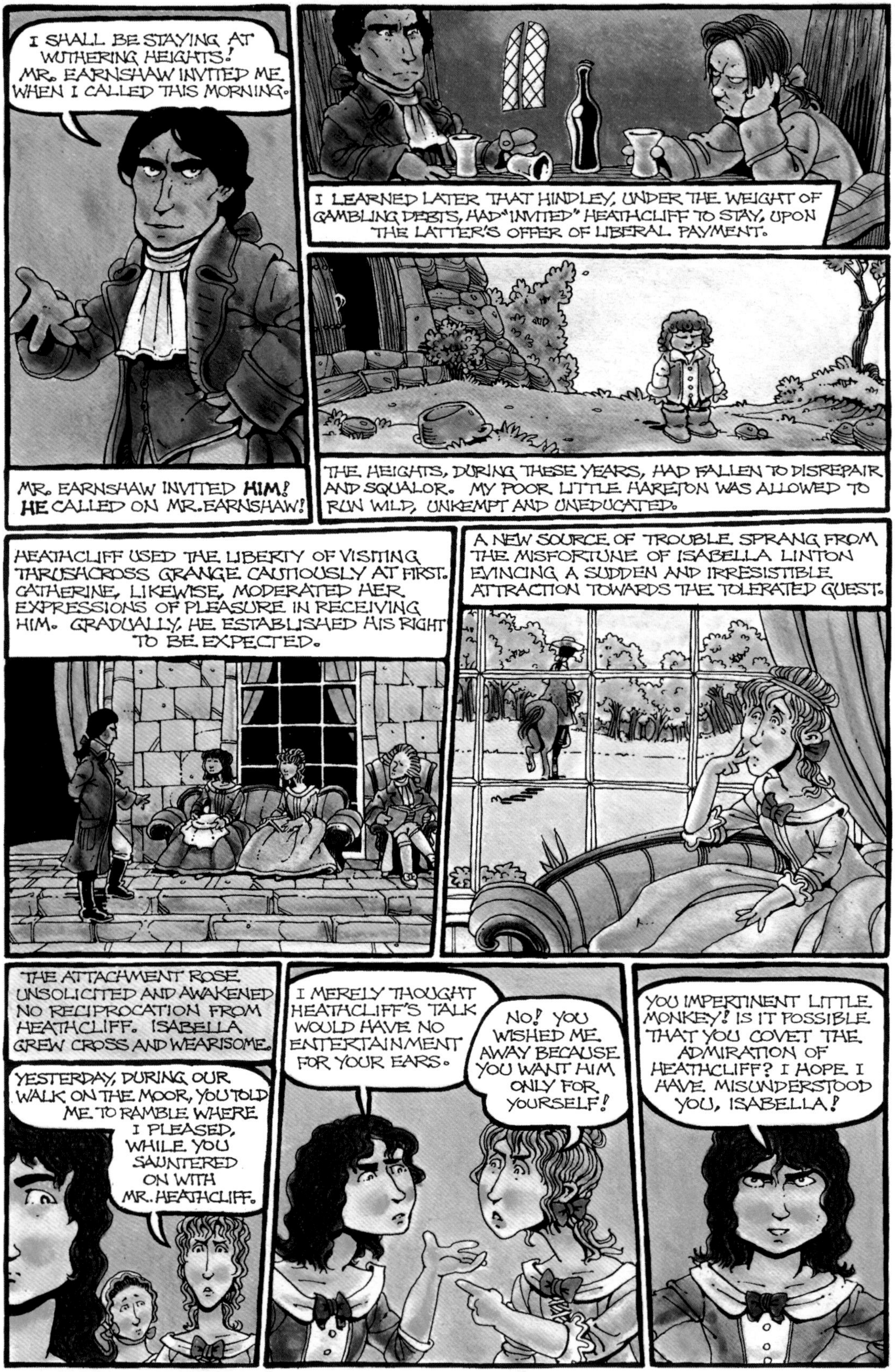
I SHALL BE STAYING AT WUTHERING HEIGHTS! MR. EARNSHAW INVITED ME WHEN I CALLED THIS MORNING.
MR. EARNSHAW INVITED HIM! HE CALLED ON MR. EARNSHAW!
I LEARNED LATER THAT HINDLEY, UNDER THE WEIGHT OF GAMBLING DEBTS, HAD "INVITED" HEATHCLIFF TO STAY, UPON THE LATTER'S OFFER OF LIBERAL PAYMENT.
THE HEIGHTS, DURING THESE YEARS, HAD FALLEN TO DISREPAIR AND SQUALOR. MY POOR LITTLE HARETON WAS ALLOWED TO RUN WILD, UNKEMPT AND UNEDUCATED.
HEATHCLIFF USED THE LIBERTY OF VISITING THRUSHCROSS GRANGE CAUTIOUSLY AT FIRST. CATHERINE, LIKEWISE, MODERATED HER EXPRESSIONS OF PLEASURE IN RECEIVING HIM. GRADUALLY, HE ESTABLISHED HIS RIGHT TO BE EXPECTED.
A NEW SOURCE OF TROUBLE SPRANG FROM THE MISFORTUNE OF ISABELLA LINTON EVINCING A SUDDEN AND IRRESISTIBLE ATTRACTION TOWARDS THE TOLERATED GUEST.
THE ATTACHMENT ROSE UNSOLICITED AND AWAKENED NO RECIPROCATION FROM HEATHCLIFF. ISABELLA GREW CROSS AND WEARISOME.
YESTERDAY, DURING OUR WALK ON THE MOOR, YOU TOLD ME TO RAMBLE WHERE I PLEASED, WHILE YOU SAUNTERED ON WITH MR. HEATHCLIFF.
I MERELY THOUGHT HEATHCLIFF'S TALK WOULD HAVE NO ENTERTAINMENT FOR YOUR EARS.
NO! YOU WISHED ME AWAY BECAUSE YOU WANT HIM ONLY FOR YOURSELF!
YOU IMPERTINENT LITTLE MONKEY! IS IT POSSIBLE THAT YOU COVET THE ADMIRATION OF HEATHCLIFF? I HOPE I HAVE MISUNDERSTOOD YOU, ISABELLA!

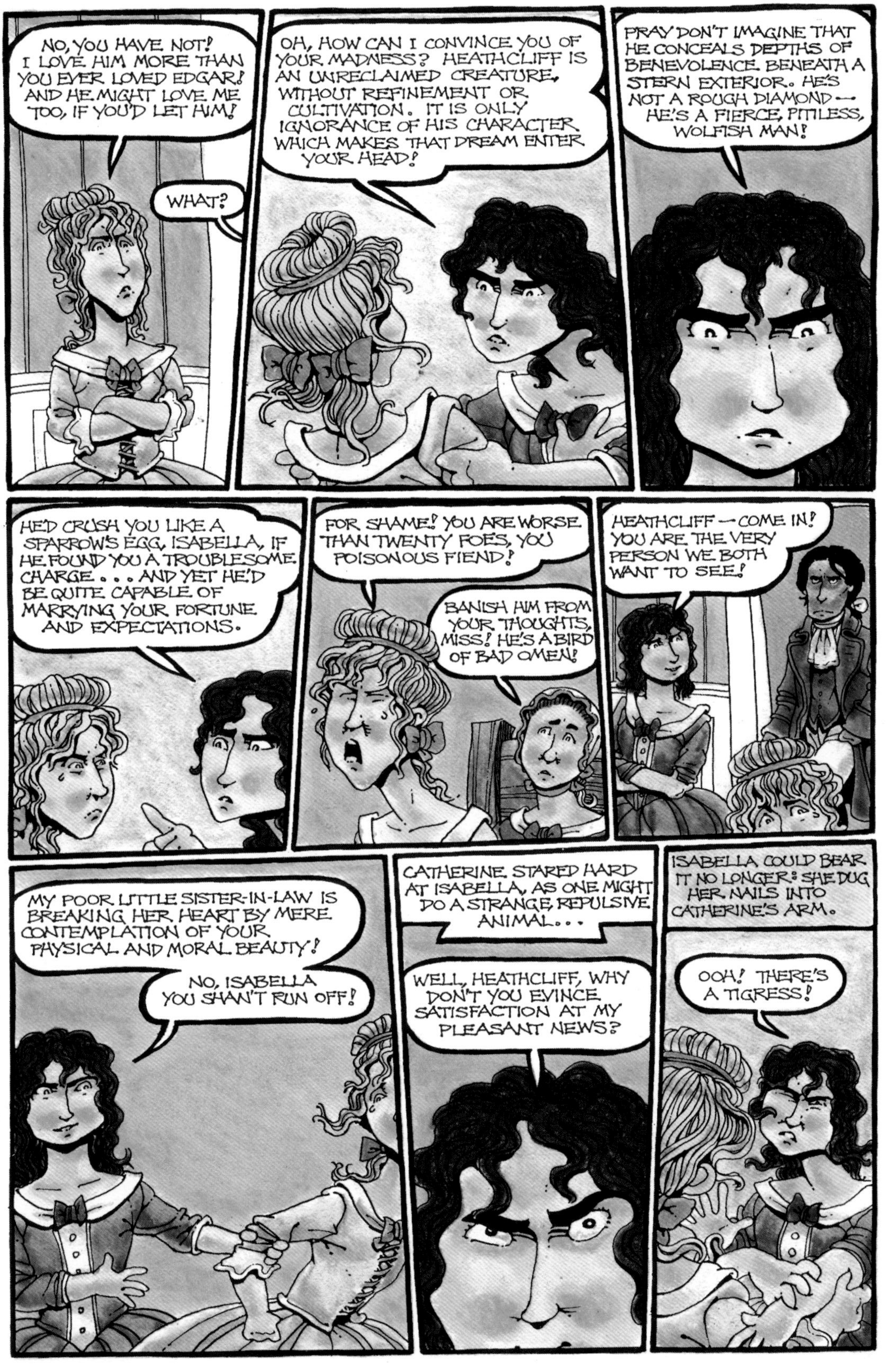
NO, YOU HAVE NOT! I LOVE HIM MORE THAN YOU EVER LOVED EDGAR! AND HE MIGHT LOVE ME TOO, IF YOU'D LET HIM!
WHAT?
OH, HOW CAN I CONVINCE YOU OF YOUR MADNESS? HEATHCLIFF IS AN UNRECLAIMED CREATURE, WITHOUT REFINEMENT OR CULTIVATION. IT IS ONLY IGNORANCE OF HIS CHARACTER WHICH MAKES THAT DREAM ENTER YOUR HEAD!
PRAY DON'T IMAGINE THAT HE CONCEALS DEPTHS OF BENEVOLENCE BENEATH A STERN EXTERIOR. HE'S NOT A ROUGH DIAMOND — HE'S A FIERCE, PITILESS, WOLFISH MAN!
HE'D CRUSH YOU LIKE A SPARROW'S EGG, ISABELLA, IF HE FOUND YOU A TROUBLESOME CHARGE . . . AND YET HE'D BE QUITE CAPABLE OF MARRYING YOUR FORTUNE AND EXPECTATIONS.
FOR SHAME! YOU ARE WORSE THAN TWENTY FOES, YOU POISONOUS FIEND!
BANISH HIM FROM YOUR THOUGHTS, MISS! HE'S A BIRD OF BAD OMEN!
HEATHCLIFF — COME IN! YOU ARE THE VERY PERSON WE BOTH WANT TO SEE!
MY POOR LITTLE SISTER-IN-LAW IS BREAKING HER HEART BY MERE CONTEMPLATION OF YOUR PHYSICAL AND MORAL BEAUTY!
NO, ISABELLA YOU SHAN'T RUN OFF!
CATHERINE STARED HARD AT ISABELLA, AS ONE MIGHT DO A STRANGE, REPULSIVE ANIMAL . . .
WELL, HEATHCLIFF, WHY DON'T YOU EVINCE SATISFACTION AT MY PLEASANT NEWS?
ISABELLA COULD BEAR IT NO LONGER: SHE DUG HER NAILS INTO CATHERINE'S ARM.
OOH! THERE'S A TIGRESS!

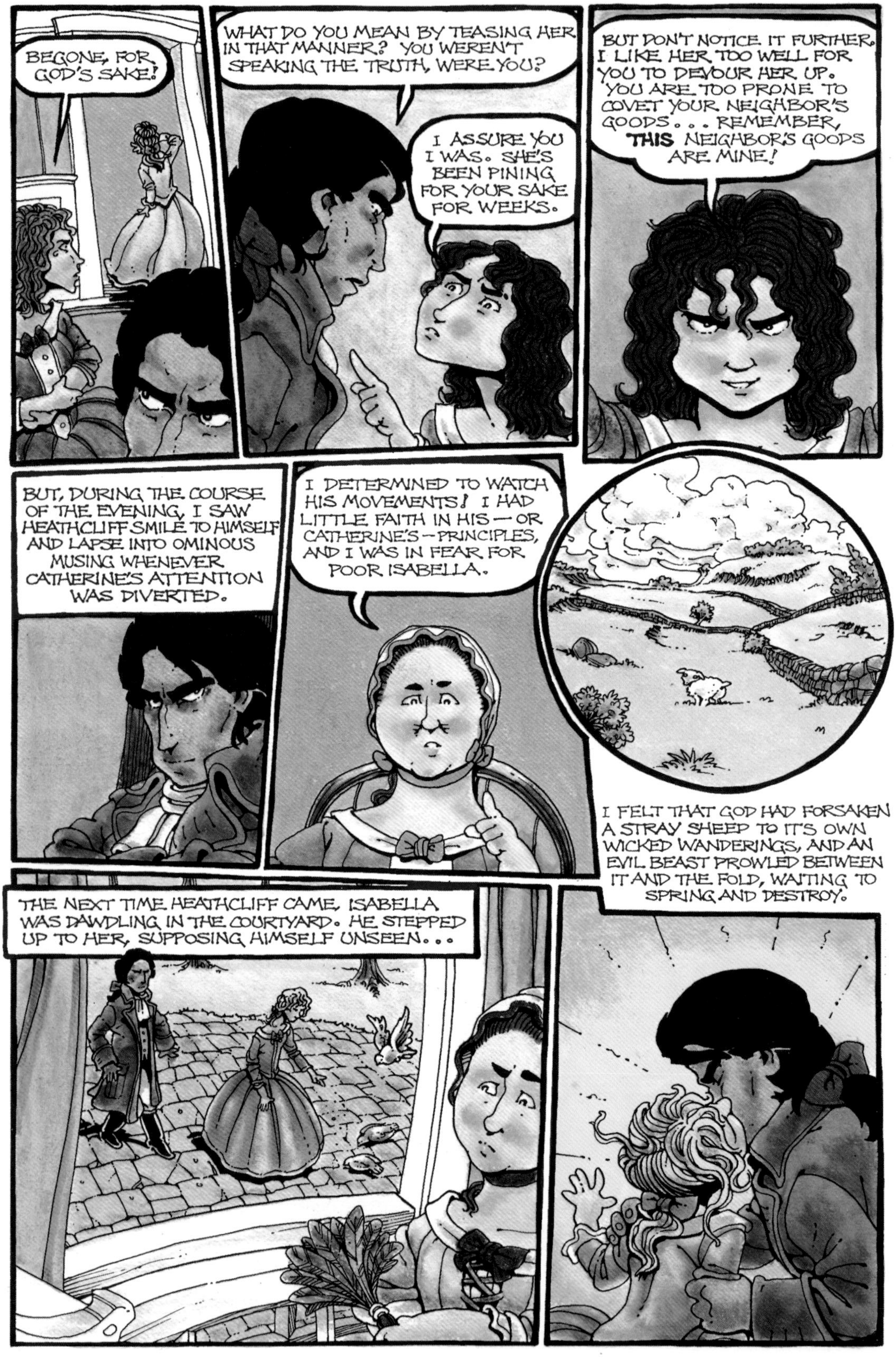
BEGONE, FOR GOD'S SAKE!
WHAT DO YOU MEAN BY TEASING HER IN THAT MANNER? YOU WEREN'T SPEAKING THE TRUTH, WERE YOU?
I ASSURE YOU I WAS. SHE'S BEEN PINING FOR YOUR SAKE FOR WEEKS.
BUT DON'T NOTICE IT FURTHER. I LIKE HER TOO WELL FOR YOU TO DEVOUR HER UP. YOU ARE TOO PRONE TO COVET YOUR NEIGHBOR'S GOODS... REMEMBER, THIS NEIGHBOR'S GOODS ARE MINE!
BUT, DURING THE COURSE OF THE EVENING, I SAW HEATHCLIFF SMILE TO HIMSELF AND LAPSE INTO OMINOUS MUSING WHENEVER CATHERINE'S ATTENTION WAS DIVERTED.
I DETERMINED TO WATCH HIS MOVEMENTS! I HAD LITTLE FAITH IN HIS — OR CATHERINE'S — PRINCIPLES, AND I WAS IN FEAR FOR POOR ISABELLA.
I FELT THAT GOD HAD FORSAKEN A STRAY SHEEP TO IT'S OWN WICKED WANDERINGS, AND AN EVIL BEAST PROWLED BETWEEN IT AND THE FOLD, WAITING TO SPRING AND DESTROY.
THE NEXT TIME HEATHCLIFF CAME, ISABELLA WAS DAWDLING IN THE COURTYARD. HE STEPPED UP TO HER, SUPPOSING HIMSELF UNSEEN...

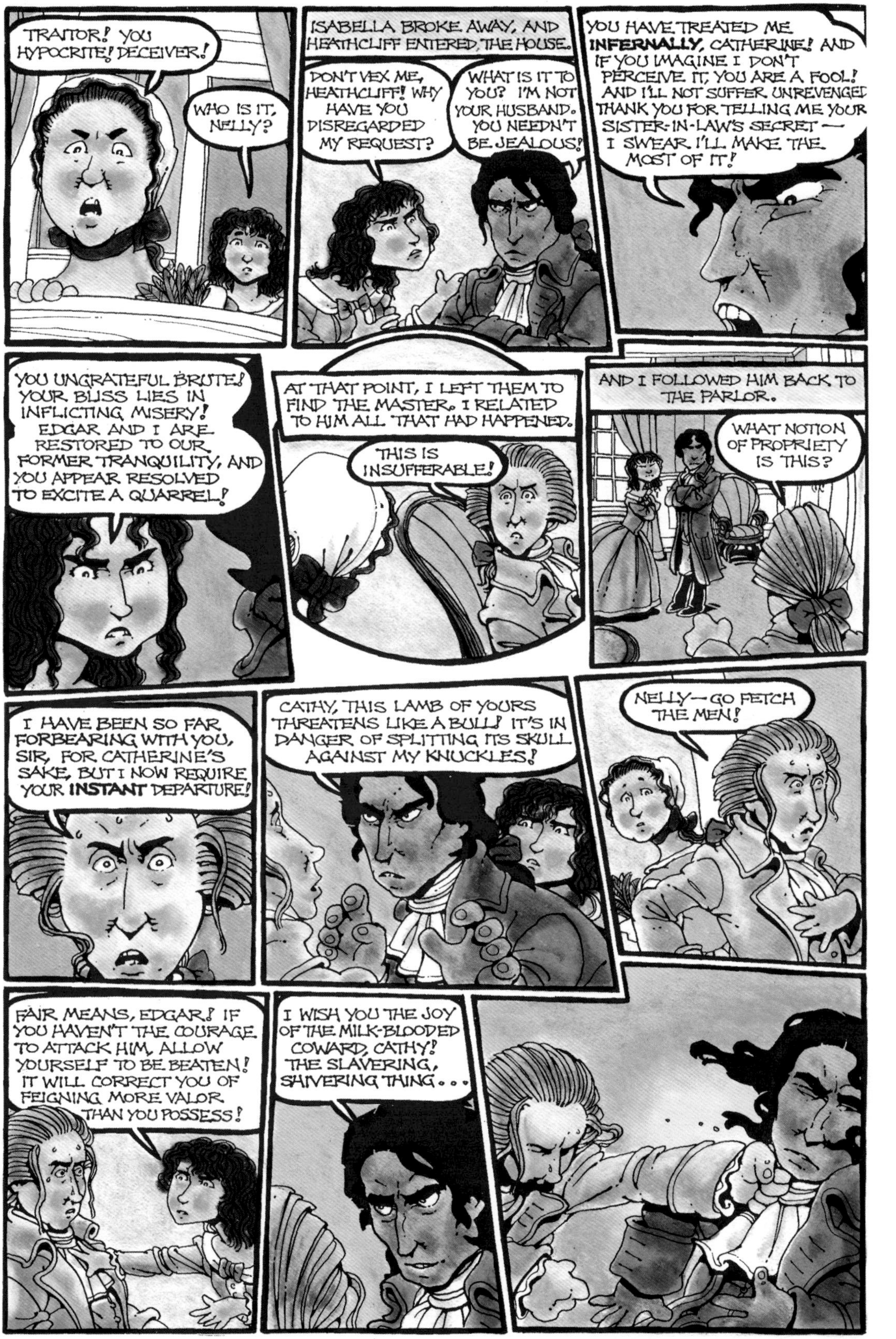
TRAITOR! YOU HYPOCRITE! DECEIVER!
WHO IS IT, NELLY?
ISABELLA BROKE AWAY, AND HEATHCLIFF ENTERED THE HOUSE.
DON'T VEX ME, HEATHCLIFF! WHY HAVE YOU DISREGARDED MY REQUEST?
WHAT IS IT TO YOU? I'M NOT YOUR HUSBAND. YOU NEEDN'T BE JEALOUS!
YOU HAVE TREATED ME **INFERNALLY**, CATHERINE! AND IF YOU IMAGINE I DON'T PERCEIVE IT, YOU ARE A FOOL! AND I'LL NOT SUFFER UNREVENGED. THANK YOU FOR TELLING ME YOUR SISTER-IN-LAW'S SECRET — I SWEAR I'LL MAKE THE MOST OF IT!
YOU UNGRATEFUL BRUTE! YOUR BLISS LIES IN INFLICTING MISERY! EDGAR AND I ARE RESTORED TO OUR FORMER TRANQUILITY, AND YOU APPEAR RESOLVED TO EXCITE A QUARREL!
AT THAT POINT, I LEFT THEM TO FIND THE MASTER. I RELATED TO HIM ALL THAT HAD HAPPENED.
THIS IS INSUFFERABLE!
AND I FOLLOWED HIM BACK TO THE PARLOR.
WHAT NOTION OF PROPRIETY IS THIS?
I HAVE BEEN SO FAR FORBEARING WITH YOU, SIR, FOR CATHERINE'S SAKE, BUT I NOW REQUIRE YOUR **INSTANT** DEPARTURE!
CATHY, THIS LAMB OF YOURS THREATENS LIKE A BULL! IT'S IN DANGER OF SPLITTING ITS SKULL AGAINST MY KNUCKLES!
NELLY — GO FETCH THE MEN!
FAIR MEANS, EDGAR! IF YOU HAVEN'T THE COURAGE TO ATTACK HIM, ALLOW YOURSELF TO BE BEATEN! IT WILL CORRECT YOU OF FEIGNING MORE VALOR THAN YOU POSSESS!
I WISH YOU THE JOY OF THE MILK-BLOODED COWARD, CATHY! THE SLAVERING, SHIVERING THING . . .

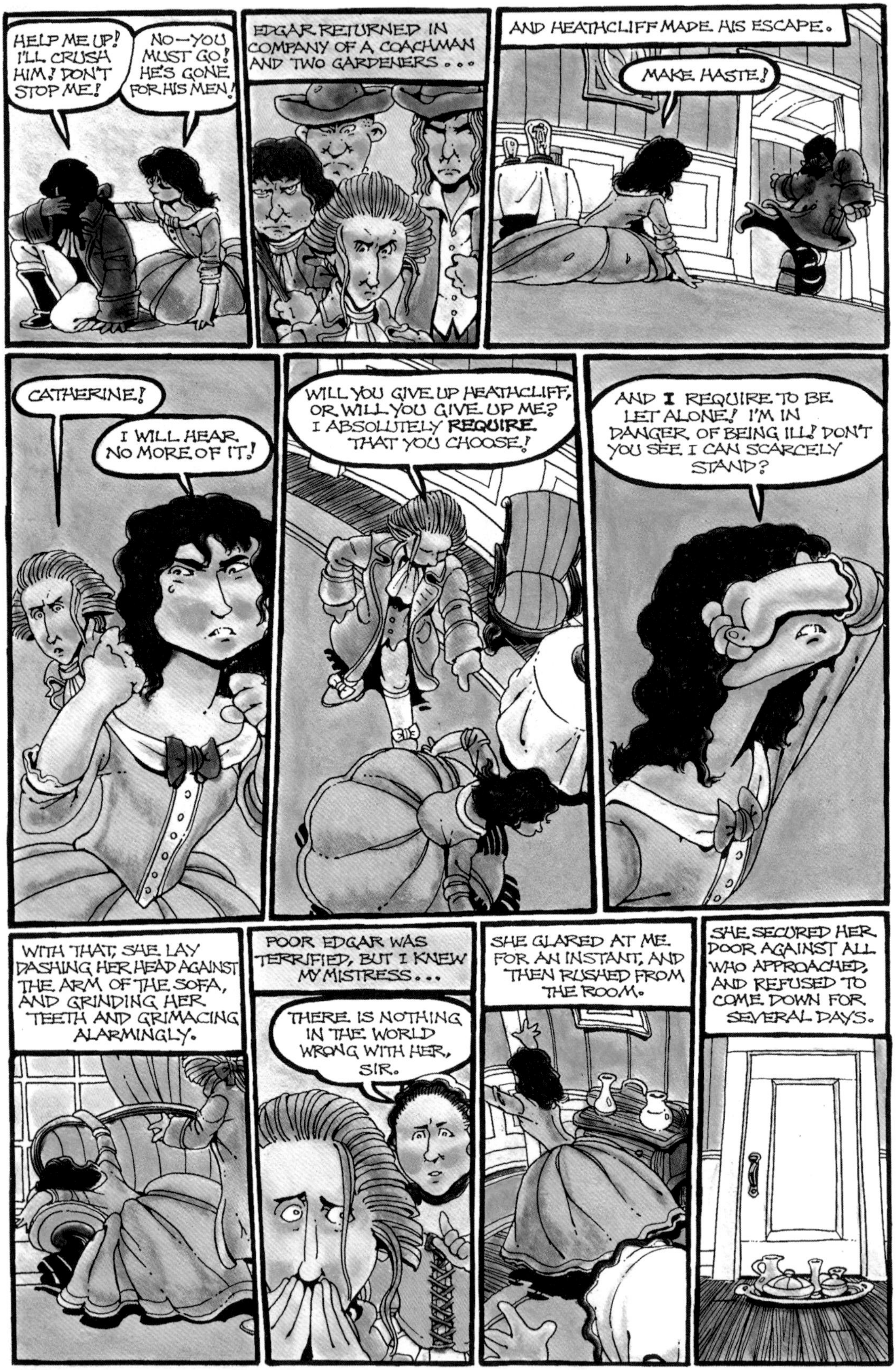
HELP ME UP! I'LL CRUSH HIM! DON'T STOP ME!
NO—YOU MUST GO! HE'S GONE FOR HIS MEN!
EDGAR RETURNED IN COMPANY OF A COACHMAN AND TWO GARDENERS . . .
AND HEATHCLIFF MADE HIS ESCAPE.
MAKE HASTE!
CATHERINE!
I WILL HEAR NO MORE OF IT!
WILL YOU GIVE UP HEATHCLIFF, OR WILL YOU GIVE UP ME? I ABSOLUTELY **REQUIRE** THAT YOU CHOOSE!
AND **I** REQUIRE TO BE LET ALONE! I'M IN DANGER OF BEING ILL! DON'T YOU SEE I CAN SCARCELY STAND?
WITH THAT, SHE LAY DASHING HER HEAD AGAINST THE ARM OF THE SOFA, AND GRINDING HER TEETH AND GRIMACING ALARMINGLY.
POOR EDGAR WAS TERRIFIED, BUT I KNEW MY MISTRESS . . .
THERE IS NOTHING IN THE WORLD WRONG WITH HER, SIR.
SHE GLARED AT ME FOR AN INSTANT, AND THEN RUSHED FROM THE ROOM.
SHE SECURED HER DOOR AGAINST ALL WHO APPROACHED, AND REFUSED TO COME DOWN FOR SEVERAL DAYS.

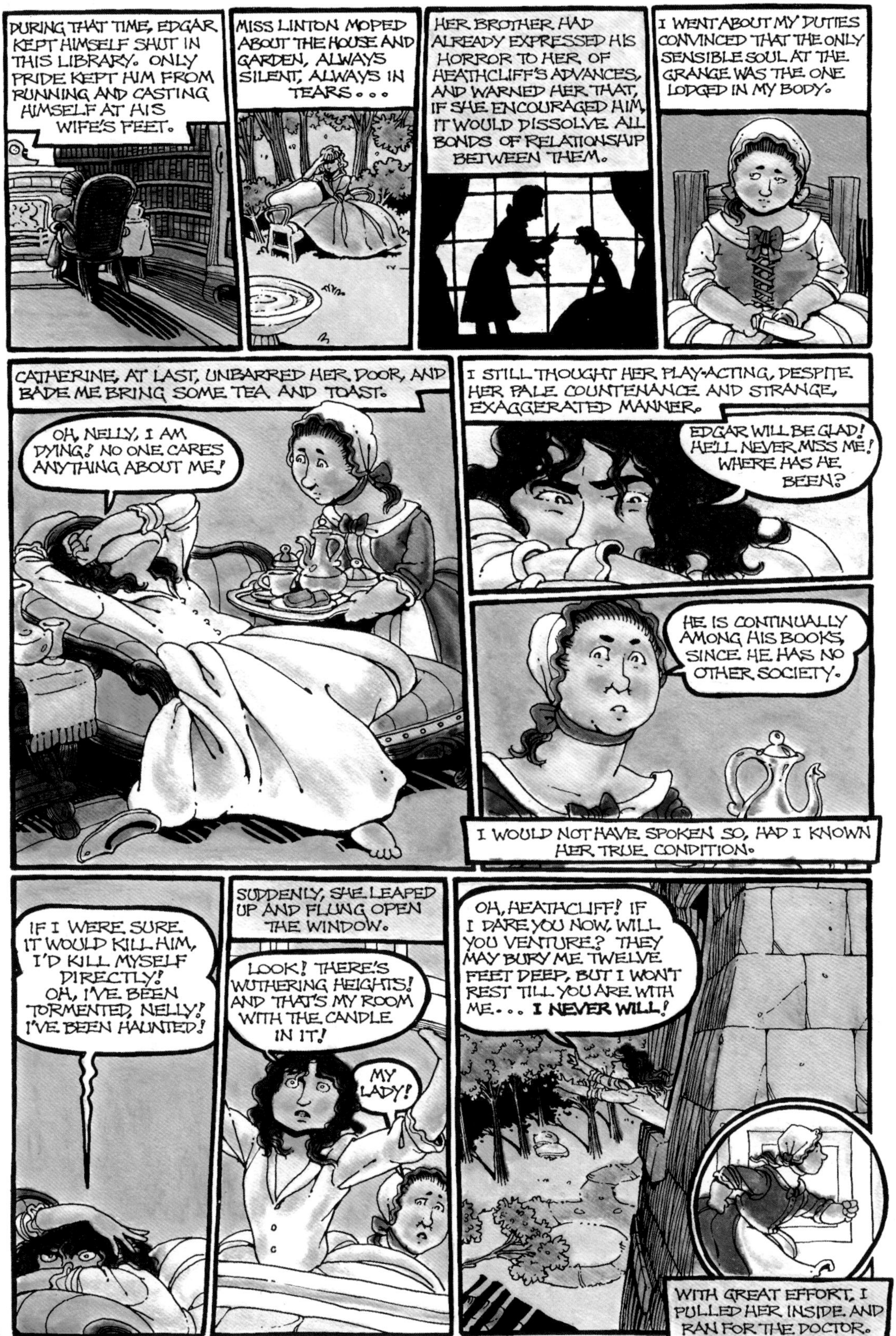
DURING THAT TIME, EDGAR KEPT HIMSELF SHUT IN THIS LIBRARY. ONLY PRIDE KEPT HIM FROM RUNNING AND CASTING HIMSELF AT HIS WIFE'S FEET.
MISS LINTON MOPED ABOUT THE HOUSE AND GARDEN, ALWAYS SILENT, ALWAYS IN TEARS...
HER BROTHER HAD ALREADY EXPRESSED HIS HORROR TO HER, OF HEATHCLIFF'S ADVANCES, AND WARNED HER THAT, IF SHE ENCOURAGED HIM, IT WOULD DISSOLVE ALL BONDS OF RELATIONSHIP BETWEEN THEM.
I WENT ABOUT MY DUTIES CONVINCED THAT THE ONLY SENSIBLE SOUL AT THE GRANGE WAS THE ONE LODGED IN MY BODY.
CATHERINE, AT LAST, UNBARRED HER DOOR, AND BADE ME BRING SOME TEA AND TOAST.
OH, NELLY, I AM DYING! NO ONE CARES ANYTHING ABOUT ME!
I STILL THOUGHT HER PLAY-ACTING, DESPITE HER PALE COUNTENANCE AND STRANGE, EXAGGERATED MANNER.
EDGAR WILL BE GLAD! HE'LL NEVER MISS ME! WHERE HAS HE BEEN?
HE IS CONTINUALLY AMONG HIS BOOKS, SINCE HE HAS NO OTHER SOCIETY.
I WOULD NOT HAVE SPOKEN SO, HAD I KNOWN HER TRUE CONDITION.
IF I WERE SURE IT WOULD KILL HIM, I'D KILL MYSELF DIRECTLY! OH, I'VE BEEN TORMENTED, NELLY! I'VE BEEN HAUNTED!
SUDDENLY, SHE LEAPED UP AND FLUNG OPEN THE WINDOW.
LOOK! THERE'S WUTHERING HEIGHTS! AND THAT'S MY ROOM WITH THE CANDLE IN IT!
MY LADY!
OH, HEATHCLIFF! IF I DARE YOU NOW, WILL YOU VENTURE? THEY MAY BURY ME TWELVE FEET DEEP, BUT I WON'T REST TILL YOU ARE WITH ME... **I NEVER WILL!**
WITH GREAT EFFORT, I PULLED HER INSIDE AND RAN FOR THE DOCTOR.

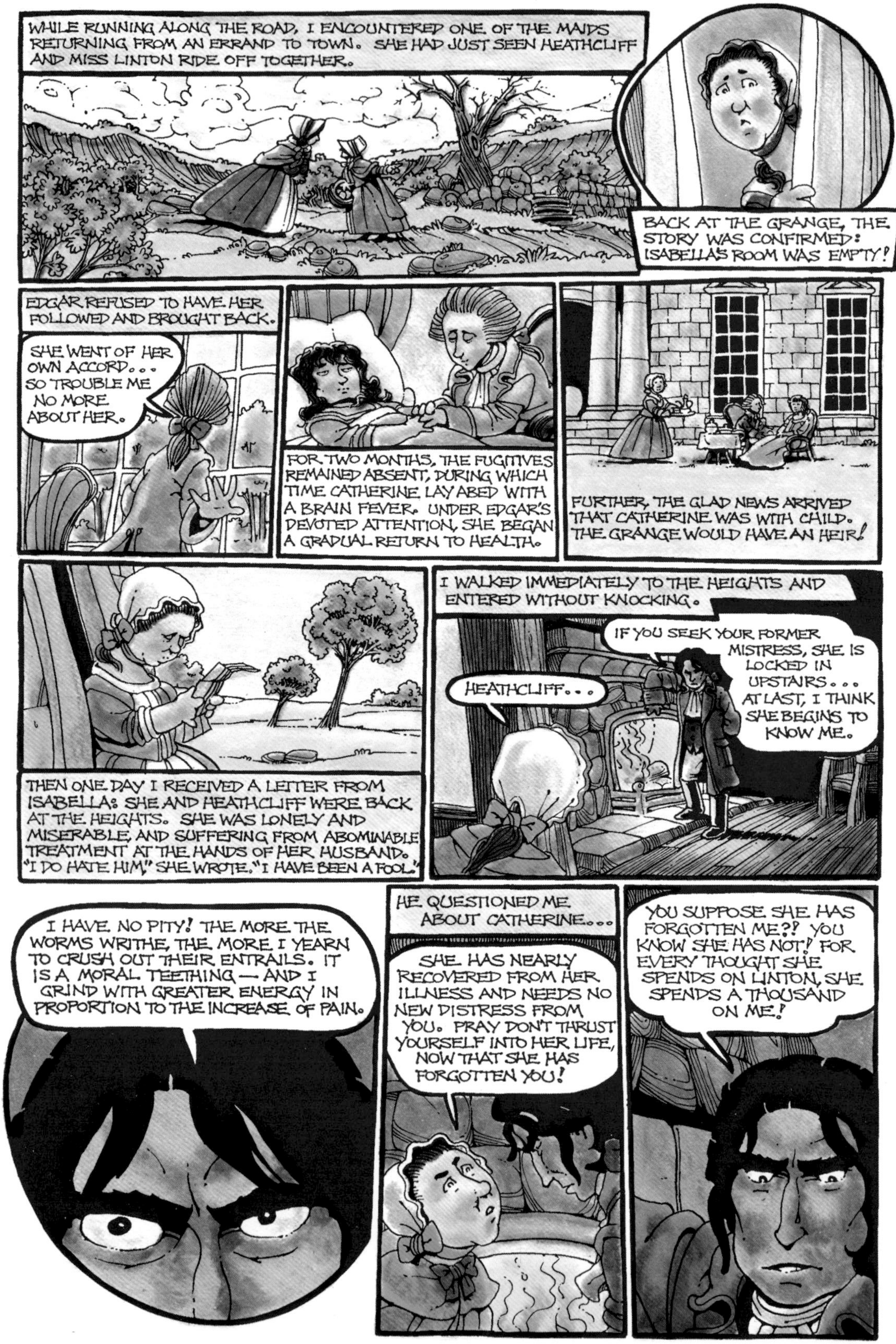
WHILE RUNNING ALONG THE ROAD, I ENCOUNTERED ONE OF THE MAIDS RETURNING FROM AN ERRAND TO TOWN. SHE HAD JUST SEEN HEATHCLIFF AND MISS LINTON RIDE OFF TOGETHER.
BACK AT THE GRANGE, THE STORY WAS CONFIRMED: ISABELLA'S ROOM WAS EMPTY!
EDGAR REFUSED TO HAVE HER FOLLOWED AND BROUGHT BACK.
SHE WENT OF HER OWN ACCORD... SO TROUBLE ME NO MORE ABOUT HER.
FOR TWO MONTHS, THE FUGITIVES REMAINED ABSENT, DURING WHICH TIME CATHERINE LAY ABED WITH A BRAIN FEVER. UNDER EDGAR'S DEVOTED ATTENTION, SHE BEGAN A GRADUAL RETURN TO HEALTH.
FURTHER, THE GLAD NEWS ARRIVED THAT CATHERINE WAS WITH CHILD. THE GRANGE WOULD HAVE AN HEIR!
THEN ONE DAY I RECEIVED A LETTER FROM ISABELLA: SHE AND HEATHCLIFF WERE BACK AT THE HEIGHTS. SHE WAS LONELY AND MISERABLE, AND SUFFERING FROM ABOMINABLE TREATMENT AT THE HANDS OF HER HUSBAND. "I DO HATE HIM," SHE WROTE. "I HAVE BEEN A FOOL."
I WALKED IMMEDIATELY TO THE HEIGHTS AND ENTERED WITHOUT KNOCKING.
HEATHCLIFF...
IF YOU SEEK YOUR FORMER MISTRESS, SHE IS LOCKED IN UPSTAIRS... AT LAST, I THINK SHE BEGINS TO KNOW ME.
I HAVE NO PITY! THE MORE THE WORMS WRITHE, THE MORE I YEARN TO CRUSH OUT THEIR ENTRAILS. IT IS A MORAL TEETHING — AND I GRIND WITH GREATER ENERGY IN PROPORTION TO THE INCREASE OF PAIN.
HE QUESTIONED ME ABOUT CATHERINE...
SHE HAS NEARLY RECOVERED FROM HER ILLNESS AND NEEDS NO NEW DISTRESS FROM YOU. PRAY DON'T THRUST YOURSELF INTO HER LIFE, NOW THAT SHE HAS FORGOTTEN YOU!
YOU SUPPOSE SHE HAS FORGOTTEN ME?! YOU KNOW SHE HAS NOT! FOR EVERY THOUGHT SHE SPENDS ON LINTON, SHE SPENDS A THOUSAND ON ME!

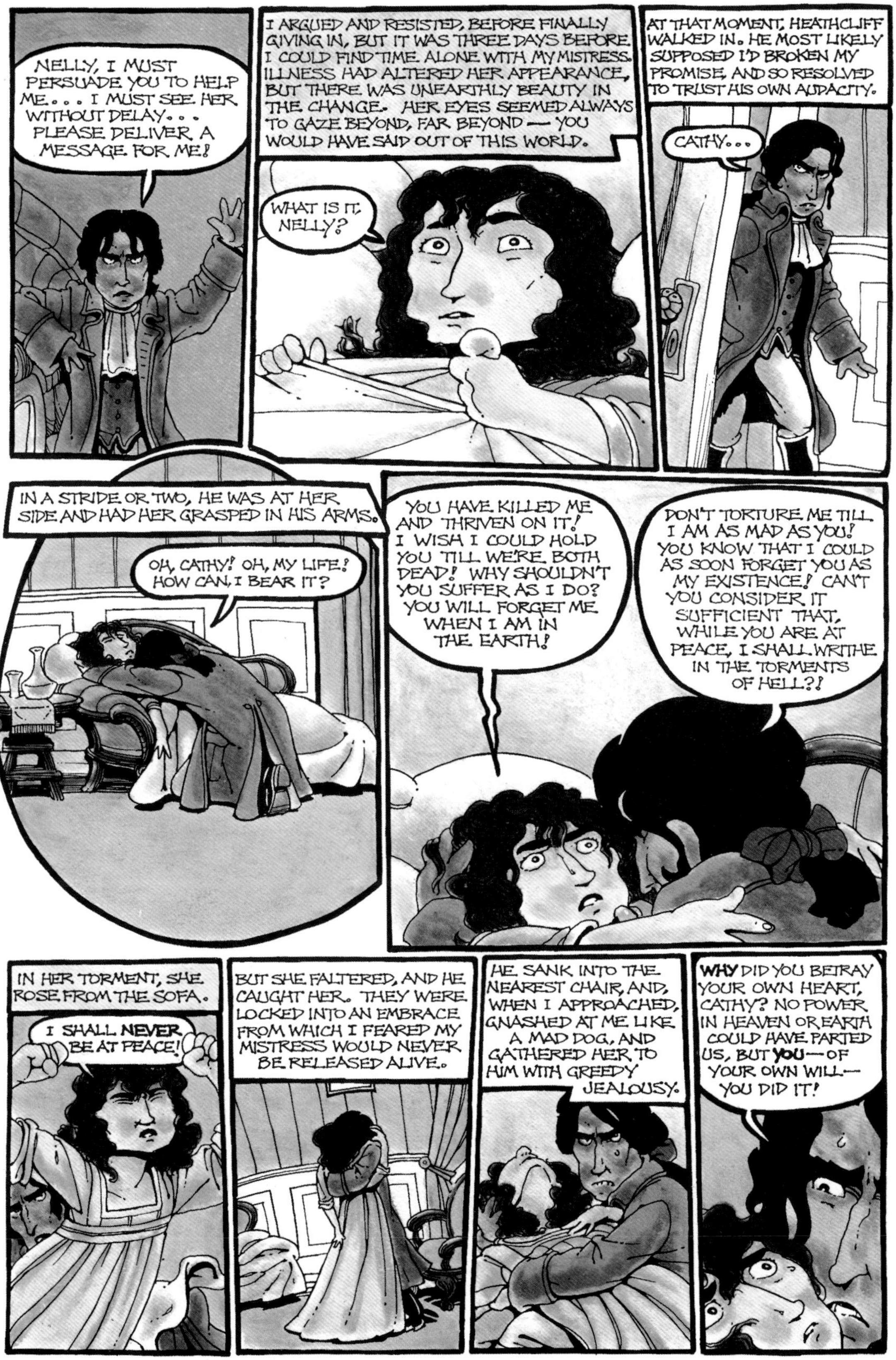
NELLY, I MUST PERSUADE YOU TO HELP ME. . . I MUST SEE HER WITHOUT DELAY. . . PLEASE DELIVER A MESSAGE FOR ME!
I ARGUED AND RESISTED, BEFORE FINALLY GIVING IN, BUT IT WAS THREE DAYS BEFORE I COULD FIND TIME ALONE WITH MY MISTRESS. ILLNESS HAD ALTERED HER APPEARANCE, BUT THERE WAS UNEARTHLY BEAUTY IN THE CHANGE. HER EYES SEEMED ALWAYS TO GAZE BEYOND, FAR BEYOND — YOU WOULD HAVE SAID OUT OF THIS WORLD.
WHAT IS IT, NELLY?
AT THAT MOMENT, HEATHCLIFF WALKED IN. HE MOST LIKELY SUPPOSED I'D BROKEN MY PROMISE, AND SO RESOLVED TO TRUST HIS OWN AUDACITY.
CATHY...
IN A STRIDE OR TWO, HE WAS AT HER SIDE AND HAD HER GRASPED IN HIS ARMS.
OH, CATHY! OH, MY LIFE! HOW CAN I BEAR IT?
YOU HAVE KILLED ME AND THRIVEN ON IT! I WISH I COULD HOLD YOU TILL WE'RE BOTH DEAD! WHY SHOULDN'T YOU SUFFER AS I DO? YOU WILL FORGET ME WHEN I AM IN THE EARTH!
DON'T TORTURE ME TILL I AM AS MAD AS YOU! YOU KNOW THAT I COULD AS SOON FORGET YOU AS MY EXISTENCE! CAN'T YOU CONSIDER IT SUFFICIENT THAT, WHILE YOU ARE AT PEACE, I SHALL WRITHE IN THE TORMENTS OF HELL?!
IN HER TORMENT, SHE ROSE FROM THE SOFA.
I SHALL NEVER BE AT PEACE!
BUT SHE FALTERED, AND HE CAUGHT HER. THEY WERE LOCKED INTO AN EMBRACE FROM WHICH I FEARED MY MISTRESS WOULD NEVER BE RELEASED ALIVE.
HE SANK INTO THE NEAREST CHAIR, AND, WHEN I APPROACHED, GNASHED AT ME LIKE A MAD DOG, AND GATHERED HER TO HIM WITH GREEDY JEALOUSY.
WHY DID YOU BETRAY YOUR OWN HEART, CATHY? NO POWER IN HEAVEN OR EARTH COULD HAVE PARTED US, BUT YOU — OF YOUR OWN WILL — YOU DID IT!

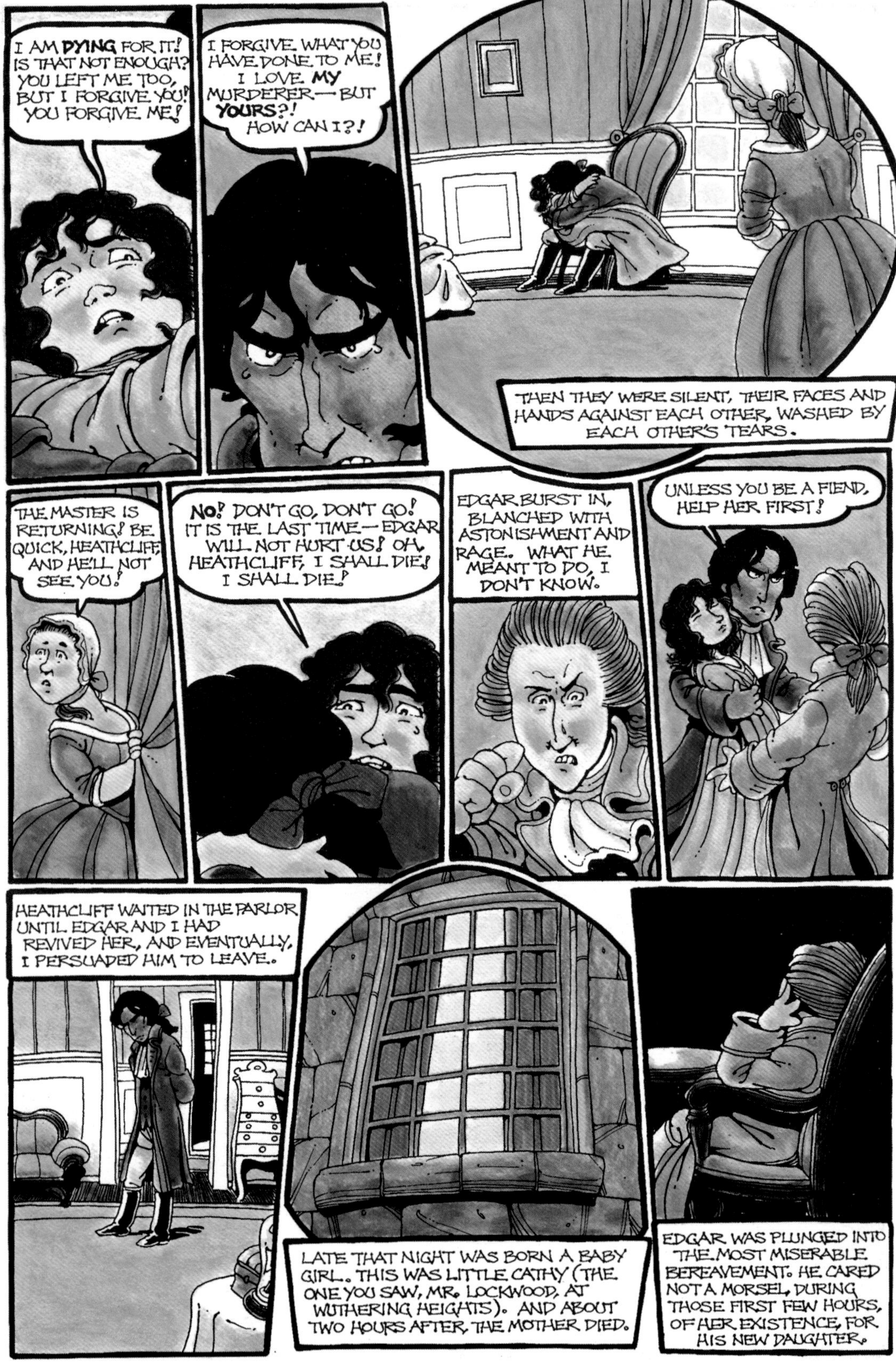

I AM **DYING** FOR IT! IS THAT NOT ENOUGH? YOU LEFT ME TOO, BUT I FORGIVE YOU! YOU FORGIVE ME!
I FORGIVE WHAT YOU HAVE DONE TO ME! I LOVE **MY** MURDERER— BUT **YOURS**?! HOW CAN I?!
THEN THEY WERE SILENT, THEIR FACES AND HANDS AGAINST EACH OTHER, WASHED BY EACH OTHER'S TEARS.
THE MASTER IS RETURNING! BE QUICK, HEATHCLIFF, AND HE'LL NOT SEE YOU!
NO! DON'T GO, DON'T GO! IT IS THE LAST TIME— EDGAR WILL NOT HURT US! OH, HEATHCLIFF, I SHALL DIE! I SHALL DIE!
EDGAR BURST IN, BLANCHED WITH ASTONISHMENT AND RAGE. WHAT HE MEANT TO DO, I DON'T KNOW.
UNLESS YOU BE A FIEND, HELP HER FIRST!
HEATHCLIFF WAITED IN THE PARLOR UNTIL EDGAR AND I HAD REVIVED HER, AND EVENTUALLY, I PERSUADED HIM TO LEAVE.
LATE THAT NIGHT WAS BORN A BABY GIRL. THIS WAS LITTLE CATHY (THE ONE YOU SAW, MR. LOCKWOOD, AT WUTHERING HEIGHTS). AND ABOUT TWO HOURS AFTER, THE MOTHER DIED.
EDGAR WAS PLUNGED INTO THE MOST MISERABLE BEREAVEMENT. HE CARED NOT A MORSEL, DURING THOSE FIRST FEW HOURS, OF HER EXISTENCE, FOR HIS NEW DAUGHTER.

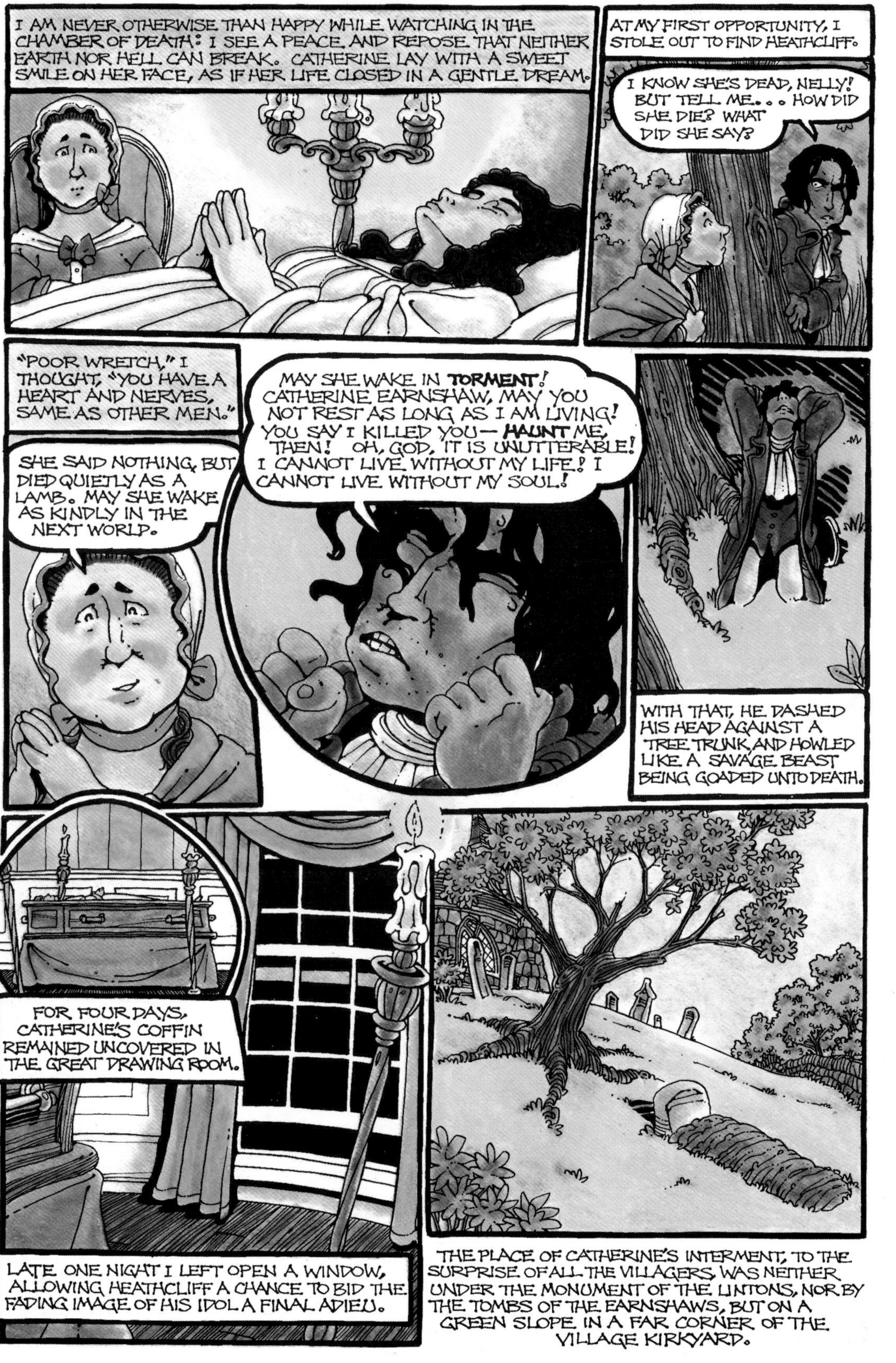

I AM NEVER OTHERWISE THAN HAPPY WHILE WATCHING IN THE CHAMBER OF DEATH: I SEE A PEACE AND REPOSE THAT NEITHER EARTH NOR HELL CAN BREAK. CATHERINE LAY WITH A SWEET SMILE ON HER FACE, AS IF HER LIFE CLOSED IN A GENTLE DREAM.
AT MY FIRST OPPORTUNITY, I STOLE OUT TO FIND HEATHCLIFF.
I KNOW SHE'S DEAD, NELLY! BUT TELL ME. . . HOW DID SHE DIE? WHAT DID SHE SAY?
"POOR WRETCH," I THOUGHT, "YOU HAVE A HEART AND NERVES, SAME AS OTHER MEN."
SHE SAID NOTHING, BUT DIED QUIETLY AS A LAMB. MAY SHE WAKE AS KINDLY IN THE NEXT WORLD.
MAY SHE WAKE IN **TORMENT**! CATHERINE EARNSHAW, MAY YOU NOT REST AS LONG AS I AM LIVING! YOU SAY I KILLED YOU— **HAUNT** ME, THEN! OH, GOD, IT IS UNUTTERABLE! I CANNOT LIVE WITHOUT MY LIFE! I CANNOT LIVE WITHOUT MY SOUL!
WITH THAT, HE DASHED HIS HEAD AGAINST A TREE TRUNK, AND HOWLED LIKE A SAVAGE BEAST BEING GOADED UNTO DEATH.
FOR FOUR DAYS, CATHERINE'S COFFIN REMAINED UNCOVERED IN THE GREAT DRAWING ROOM.
LATE ONE NIGHT I LEFT OPEN A WINDOW, ALLOWING HEATHCLIFF A CHANCE TO BID THE FADING IMAGE OF HIS IDOL A FINAL ADIEU.
THE PLACE OF CATHERINE'S INTERMENT, TO THE SURPRISE OF ALL THE VILLAGERS, WAS NEITHER UNDER THE MONUMENT OF THE LINTONS, NOR BY THE TOMBS OF THE EARNSHAWS, BUT ON A GREEN SLOPE IN A FAR CORNER OF THE VILLAGE KIRKYARD.

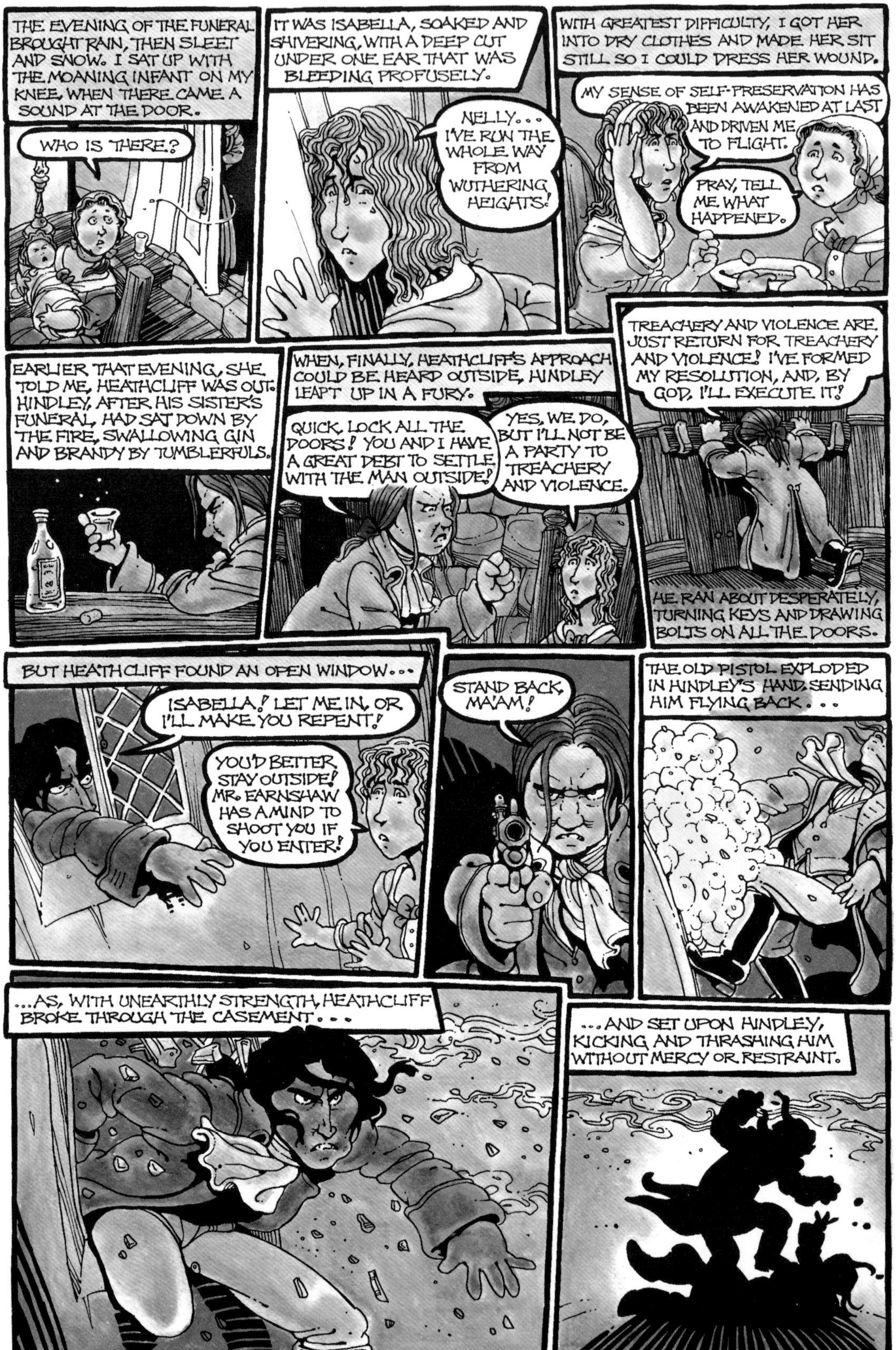
THE EVENING OF THE FUNERAL BROUGHT RAIN, THEN SLEET AND SNOW. I SAT UP WITH THE MOANING INFANT ON MY KNEE, WHEN THERE CAME A SOUND AT THE DOOR.
WHO IS THERE?
IT WAS ISABELLA, SOAKED AND SHIVERING, WITH A DEEP CUT UNDER ONE EAR THAT WAS BLEEDING PROFUSELY.
NELLY... I'VE RUN THE WHOLE WAY FROM WUTHERING HEIGHTS!
WITH GREATEST DIFFICULTY, I GOT HER INTO DRY CLOTHES AND MADE HER SIT STILL SO I COULD DRESS HER WOUND.
MY SENSE OF SELF-PRESERVATION HAS BEEN AWAKENED AT LAST AND DRIVEN ME TO FLIGHT.
PRAY, TELL ME WHAT HAPPENED.
EARLIER THAT EVENING, SHE TOLD ME, HEATHCLIFF WAS OUT. HINDLEY, AFTER HIS SISTER'S FUNERAL, HAD SAT DOWN BY THE FIRE, SWALLOWING GIN AND BRANDY BY TUMBLERFULS.
WHEN, FINALLY, HEATHCLIFF'S APPROACH COULD BE HEARD OUTSIDE, HINDLEY LEAPT UP IN A FURY.
QUICK, LOCK ALL THE DOORS! YOU AND I HAVE A GREAT DEBT TO SETTLE WITH THE MAN OUTSIDE!
YES, WE DO, BUT I'LL NOT BE A PARTY TO TREACHERY AND VIOLENCE.
TREACHERY AND VIOLENCE ARE JUST RETURN FOR TREACHERY AND VIOLENCE! I'VE FORMED MY RESOLUTION, AND, BY GOD, I'LL EXECUTE IT!
HE RAN ABOUT DESPERATELY, TURNING KEYS AND DRAWING BOLTS ON ALL THE DOORS.
BUT HEATHCLIFF FOUND AN OPEN WINDOW...
ISABELLA! LET ME IN, OR I'LL MAKE YOU REPENT!
YOU'D BETTER STAY OUTSIDE! MR. EARNSHAW HAS A MIND TO SHOOT YOU IF YOU ENTER!
STAND BACK, MA'AM!
THE OLD PISTOL EXPLODED IN HINDLEY'S HAND, SENDING HIM FLYING BACK...
...AS, WITH UNEARTHLY STRENGTH, HEATHCLIFF BROKE THROUGH THE CASEMENT...
...AND SET UPON HINDLEY, KICKING AND THRASHING HIM WITHOUT MERCY OR RESTRAINT.

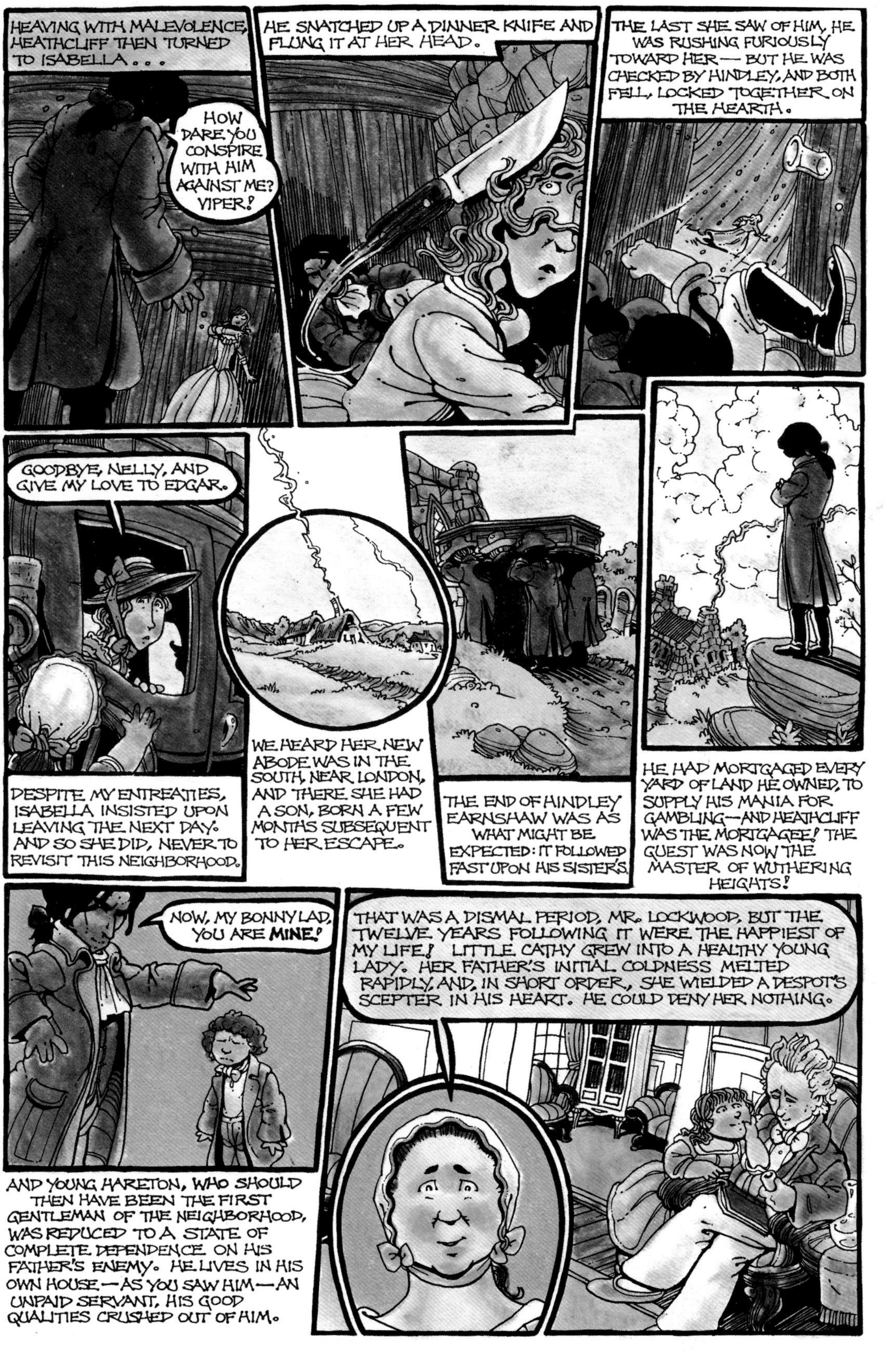
HEAVING WITH MALEVOLENCE, HEATHCLIFF THEN TURNED TO ISABELLA . . .
HOW DARE YOU CONSPIRE WITH HIM AGAINST ME? VIPER!
HE SNATCHED UP A DINNER KNIFE AND FLUNG IT AT HER HEAD.
THE LAST SHE SAW OF HIM, HE WAS RUSHING FURIOUSLY TOWARD HER— BUT HE WAS CHECKED BY HINDLEY, AND BOTH FELL, LOCKED TOGETHER ON THE HEARTH.
GOODBYE, NELLY, AND GIVE MY LOVE TO EDGAR.
DESPITE MY ENTREATIES, ISABELLA INSISTED UPON LEAVING THE NEXT DAY. AND SO SHE DID, NEVER TO REVISIT THIS NEIGHBORHOOD.
WE HEARD HER NEW ABODE WAS IN THE SOUTH, NEAR LONDON, AND THERE SHE HAD A SON, BORN A FEW MONTHS SUBSEQUENT TO HER ESCAPE.
THE END OF HINDLEY EARNSHAW WAS AS WHAT MIGHT BE EXPECTED: IT FOLLOWED FAST UPON HIS SISTER'S.
HE HAD MORTGAGED EVERY YARD OF LAND HE OWNED, TO SUPPLY HIS MANIA FOR GAMBLING—AND HEATHCLIFF WAS THE MORTGAGEE! THE GUEST WAS NOW THE MASTER OF WUTHERING HEIGHTS!
NOW, MY BONNY LAD, YOU ARE **MINE**!
AND YOUNG HARETON, WHO SHOULD THEN HAVE BEEN THE FIRST GENTLEMAN OF THE NEIGHBORHOOD, WAS REDUCED TO A STATE OF COMPLETE DEPENDENCE ON HIS FATHER'S ENEMY. HE LIVES IN HIS OWN HOUSE—AS YOU SAW HIM—AN UNPAID SERVANT, HIS GOOD QUALITIES CRUSHED OUT OF HIM.
THAT WAS A DISMAL PERIOD, MR. LOCKWOOD, BUT THE TWELVE YEARS FOLLOWING IT WERE THE HAPPIEST OF MY LIFE! LITTLE CATHY GREW INTO A HEALTHY YOUNG LADY. HER FATHER'S INITIAL COLDNESS MELTED RAPIDLY, AND, IN SHORT ORDER, SHE WIELDED A DESPOT'S SCEPTER IN HIS HEART. HE COULD DENY HER NOTHING.

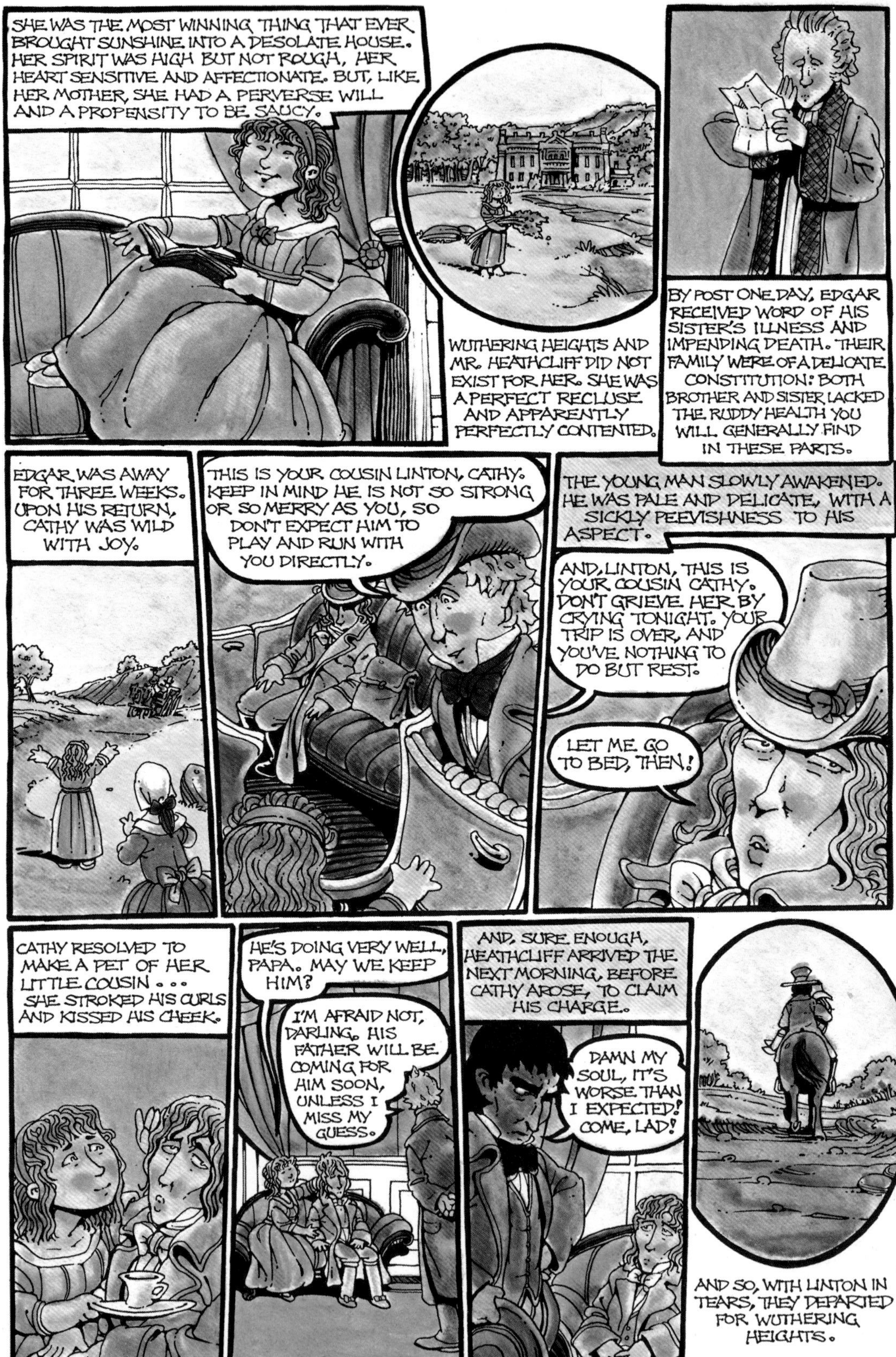

SHE WAS THE MOST WINNING THING THAT EVER BROUGHT SUNSHINE INTO A DESOLATE HOUSE. HER SPIRIT WAS HIGH BUT NOT ROUGH, HER HEART SENSITIVE AND AFFECTIONATE. BUT, LIKE HER MOTHER, SHE HAD A PERVERSE WILL AND A PROPENSITY TO BE SAUCY.
WUTHERING HEIGHTS AND MR. HEATHCLIFF DID NOT EXIST FOR HER. SHE WAS A PERFECT RECLUSE AND APPARENTLY PERFECTLY CONTENTED.
BY POST ONE DAY, EDGAR RECEIVED WORD OF HIS SISTER'S ILLNESS AND IMPENDING DEATH. THEIR FAMILY WERE OF A DELICATE CONSTITUTION: BOTH BROTHER AND SISTER LACKED THE RUDDY HEALTH YOU WILL GENERALLY FIND IN THESE PARTS.
EDGAR WAS AWAY FOR THREE WEEKS. UPON HIS RETURN, CATHY WAS WILD WITH JOY.
THIS IS YOUR COUSIN LINTON, CATHY. KEEP IN MIND HE IS NOT SO STRONG OR SO MERRY AS YOU, SO DON'T EXPECT HIM TO PLAY AND RUN WITH YOU DIRECTLY.
THE YOUNG MAN SLOWLY AWAKENED. HE WAS PALE AND DELICATE, WITH A SICKLY PEEVISHNESS TO HIS ASPECT.
AND, LINTON, THIS IS YOUR COUSIN CATHY. DON'T GRIEVE HER BY CRYING TONIGHT. YOUR TRIP IS OVER, AND YOU'VE NOTHING TO DO BUT REST.
LET ME GO TO BED, THEN!
CATHY RESOLVED TO MAKE A PET OF HER LITTLE COUSIN . . . SHE STROKED HIS CURLS AND KISSED HIS CHEEK.
HE'S DOING VERY WELL, PAPA. MAY WE KEEP HIM?
I'M AFRAID NOT, DARLING. HIS FATHER WILL BE COMING FOR HIM SOON, UNLESS I MISS MY GUESS.
AND, SURE ENOUGH, HEATHCLIFF ARRIVED THE NEXT MORNING, BEFORE CATHY AROSE, TO CLAIM HIS CHARGE.
DAMN MY SOUL, IT'S WORSE THAN I EXPECTED! COME, LAD!
AND SO, WITH LINTON IN TEARS, THEY DEPARTED FOR WUTHERING HEIGHTS.

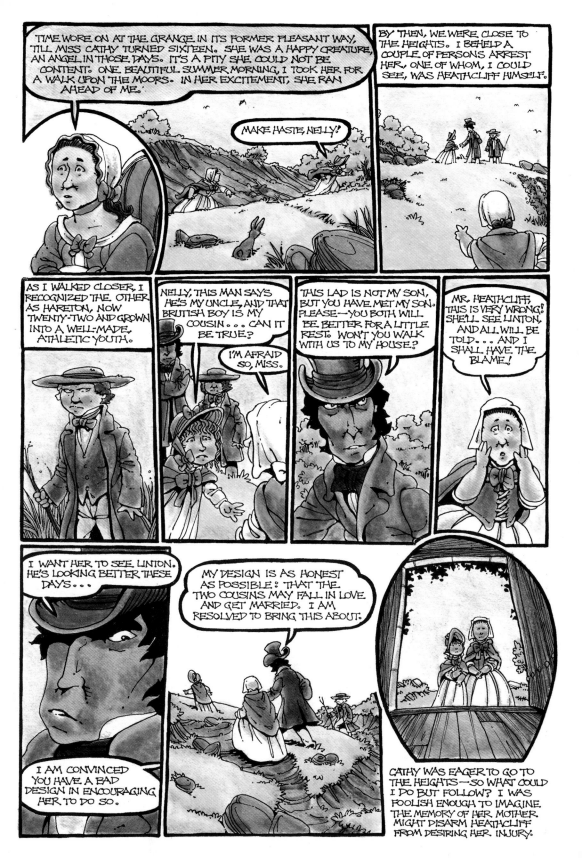

TIME WORE ON AT THE GRANGE IN ITS FORMER PLEASANT WAY, 'TILL MISS CATHY TURNED SIXTEEN. SHE WAS A HAPPY CREATURE, AN ANGEL IN THOSE DAYS. IT'S A PITY SHE COULD NOT BE CONTENT. ONE BEAUTIFUL SUMMER MORNING, I TOOK HER FOR A WALK UPON THE MOORS. IN HER EXCITEMENT, SHE RAN AHEAD OF ME.

MAKE HASTE, NELLY!

BY THEN, WE WERE CLOSE TO THE HEIGHTS. I BEHELD A COUPLE OF PERSONS ARREST HER, ONE OF WHOM, I COULD SEE, WAS HEATHCLIFF HIMSELF.

AS I WALKED CLOSER, I RECOGNIZED THE OTHER AS HARETON, NOW TWENTY-TWO AND GROWN INTO A WELL-MADE, ATHLETIC YOUTH.

NELLY, THIS MAN SAYS HE'S MY UNCLE, AND THAT BRUTISH BOY IS MY COUSIN... CAN IT BE TRUE?

I'M AFRAID SO, MISS.

THIS LAD IS NOT MY SON, BUT YOU HAVE MET MY SON. PLEASE—YOU BOTH WILL BE BETTER FOR A LITTLE REST. WON'T YOU WALK WITH US TO MY HOUSE?

MR. HEATHCLIFF, THIS IS VERY WRONG! SHE'LL SEE LINTON, AND ALL WILL BE TOLD... AND I SHALL HAVE THE BLAME!

I WANT HER TO SEE LINTON. HE'S LOOKING BETTER THESE DAYS...

MY DESIGN IS AS HONEST AS POSSIBLE: THAT THE TWO COUSINS MAY FALL IN LOVE AND GET MARRIED. I AM RESOLVED TO BRING THIS ABOUT.

I AM CONVINCED YOU HAVE A BAD DESIGN IN ENCOURAGING HER TO DO SO.

CATHY WAS EAGER TO GO TO THE HEIGHTS—SO WHAT COULD I DO BUT FOLLOW? I WAS FOOLISH ENOUGH TO IMAGINE THE MEMORY OF HER MOTHER MIGHT DISARM HEATHCLIFF FROM DESIRING HER INJURY.

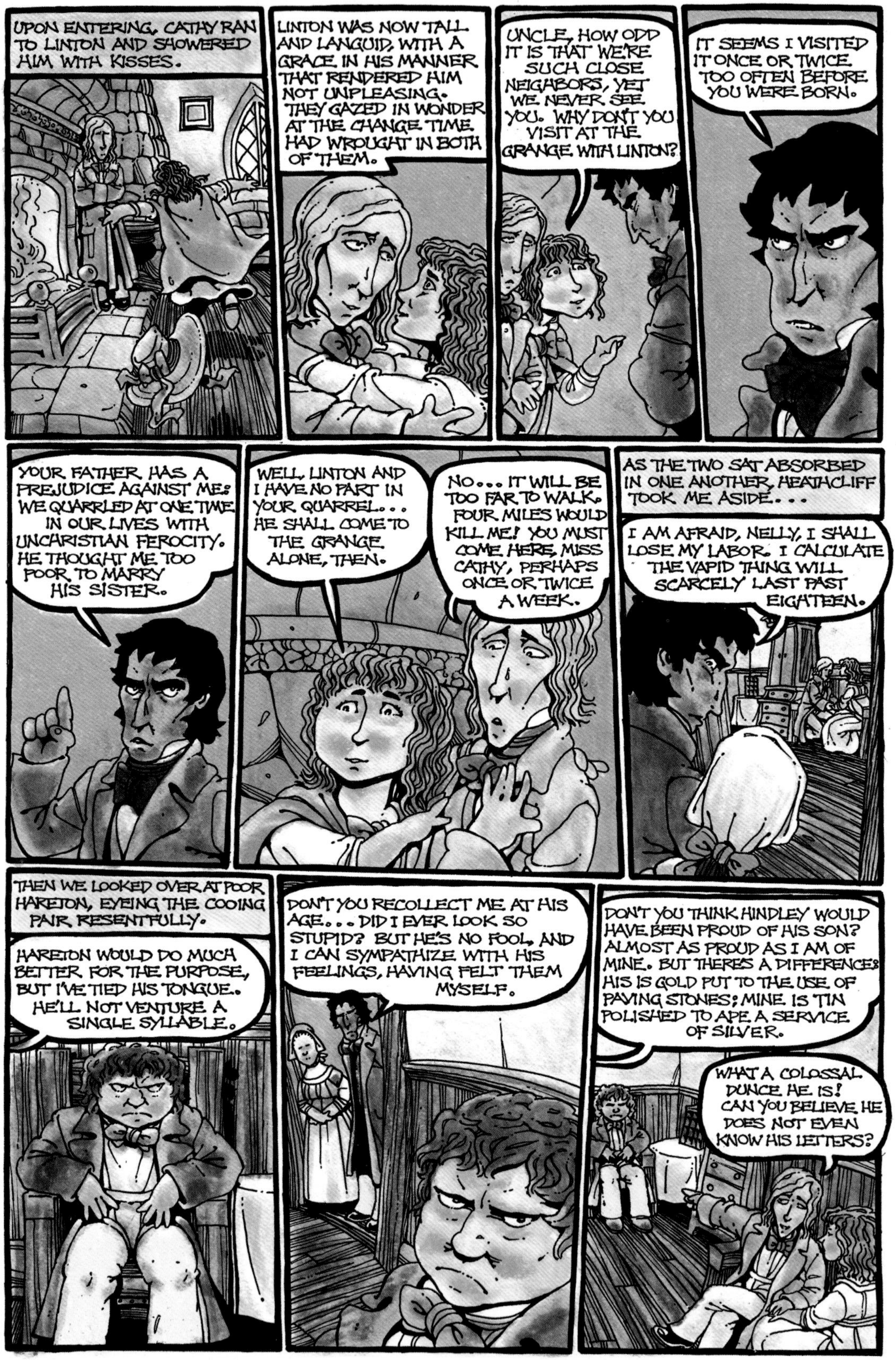

UPON ENTERING, CATHY RAN TO LINTON AND SHOWERED HIM WITH KISSES.
LINTON WAS NOW TALL AND LANGUID, WITH A GRACE IN HIS MANNER THAT RENDERED HIM NOT UNPLEASING. THEY GAZED IN WONDER AT THE CHANGE TIME HAD WROUGHT IN BOTH OF THEM.
UNCLE, HOW ODD IT IS THAT WE'RE SUCH CLOSE NEIGHBORS, YET WE NEVER SEE YOU. WHY DON'T YOU VISIT AT THE GRANGE WITH LINTON?
IT SEEMS I VISITED IT ONCE OR TWICE TOO OFTEN BEFORE YOU WERE BORN.
YOUR FATHER HAS A PREJUDICE AGAINST ME: WE QUARRLED AT ONE TIME IN OUR LIVES WITH UNCHRISTIAN FEROCITY. HE THOUGHT ME TOO POOR TO MARRY HIS SISTER.
WELL, LINTON AND I HAVE NO PART IN YOUR QUARREL... HE SHALL COME TO THE GRANGE ALONE, THEN.
NO... IT WILL BE TOO FAR TO WALK. FOUR MILES WOULD KILL ME! YOU MUST COME HERE, MISS CATHY, PERHAPS ONCE OR TWICE A WEEK.
AS THE TWO SAT ABSORBED IN ONE ANOTHER, HEATHCLIFF TOOK ME ASIDE...
I AM AFRAID, NELLY, I SHALL LOSE MY LABOR. I CALCULATE THE VAPID THING WILL SCARCELY LAST PAST EIGHTEEN.
THEN WE LOOKED OVER AT POOR HARETON, EYEING THE COOING PAIR RESENTFULLY.
HARETON WOULD DO MUCH BETTER FOR THE PURPOSE, BUT I'VE TIED HIS TONGUE. HE'LL NOT VENTURE A SINGLE SYLLABLE.
DON'T YOU RECOLLECT ME AT HIS AGE... DID I EVER LOOK SO STUPID? BUT HE'S NO FOOL, AND I CAN SYMPATHIZE WITH HIS FEELINGS, HAVING FELT THEM MYSELF.
DON'T YOU THINK HINDLEY WOULD HAVE BEEN PROUD OF HIS SON? ALMOST AS PROUD AS I AM OF MINE. BUT THERE'S A DIFFERENCE: HIS IS GOLD PUT TO THE USE OF PAVING STONES; MINE IS TIN POLISHED TO APE A SERVICE OF SILVER.
WHAT A COLOSSAL DUNCE HE IS! CAN YOU BELIEVE HE DOES NOT EVEN KNOW HIS LETTERS?

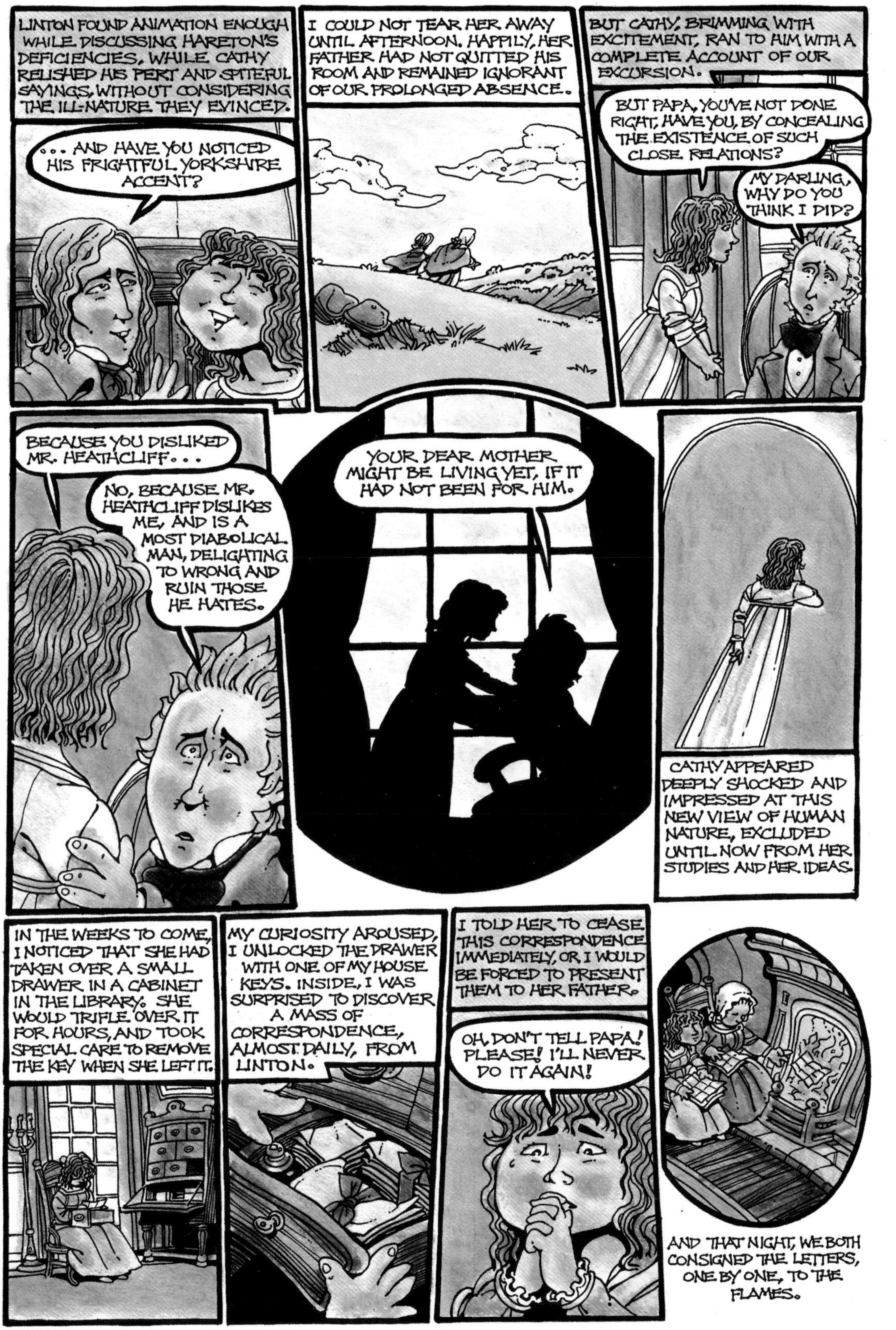
LINTON FOUND ANIMATION ENOUGH WHILE DISCUSSING HARETON'S DEFICIENCIES, WHILE CATHY RELISHED HIS PERT AND SPITEFUL SAYINGS, WITHOUT CONSIDERING THE ILL-NATURE THEY EVINCED.
... AND HAVE YOU NOTICED HIS FRIGHTFUL YORKSHIRE ACCENT?
I COULD NOT TEAR HER AWAY UNTIL AFTERNOON. HAPPILY, HER FATHER HAD NOT QUITTED HIS ROOM AND REMAINED IGNORANT OF OUR PROLONGED ABSENCE.
BUT CATHY, BRIMMING WITH EXCITEMENT, RAN TO HIM WITH A COMPLETE ACCOUNT OF OUR EXCURSION.
BUT PAPA, YOU'VE NOT DONE RIGHT, HAVE YOU, BY CONCEALING THE EXISTENCE OF SUCH CLOSE RELATIONS?
MY DARLING, WHY DO YOU THINK I DID?
BECAUSE YOU DISLIKED MR. HEATHCLIFF...
NO, BECAUSE MR. HEATHCLIFF DISLIKES ME, AND IS A MOST DIABOLICAL MAN, DELIGHTING TO WRONG AND RUIN THOSE HE HATES.
YOUR DEAR MOTHER MIGHT BE LIVING YET, IF IT HAD NOT BEEN FOR HIM.
CATHY APPEARED DEEPLY SHOCKED AND IMPRESSED AT THIS NEW VIEW OF HUMAN NATURE, EXCLUDED UNTIL NOW FROM HER STUDIES AND HER IDEAS.
IN THE WEEKS TO COME, I NOTICED THAT SHE HAD TAKEN OVER A SMALL DRAWER IN A CABINET IN THE LIBRARY. SHE WOULD TRIFLE OVER IT FOR HOURS, AND TOOK SPECIAL CARE TO REMOVE THE KEY WHEN SHE LEFT IT.
MY CURIOSITY AROUSED, I UNLOCKED THE DRAWER WITH ONE OF MY HOUSE KEYS. INSIDE, I WAS SURPRISED TO DISCOVER A MASS OF CORRESPONDENCE, ALMOST DAILY, FROM LINTON.
I TOLD HER TO CEASE THIS CORRESPONDENCE IMMEDIATELY, OR I WOULD BE FORCED TO PRESENT THEM TO HER FATHER.
OH, DON'T TELL PAPA! PLEASE! I'LL NEVER DO IT AGAIN!
AND THAT NIGHT, WE BOTH CONSIGNED THE LETTERS, ONE BY ONE, TO THE FLAMES.

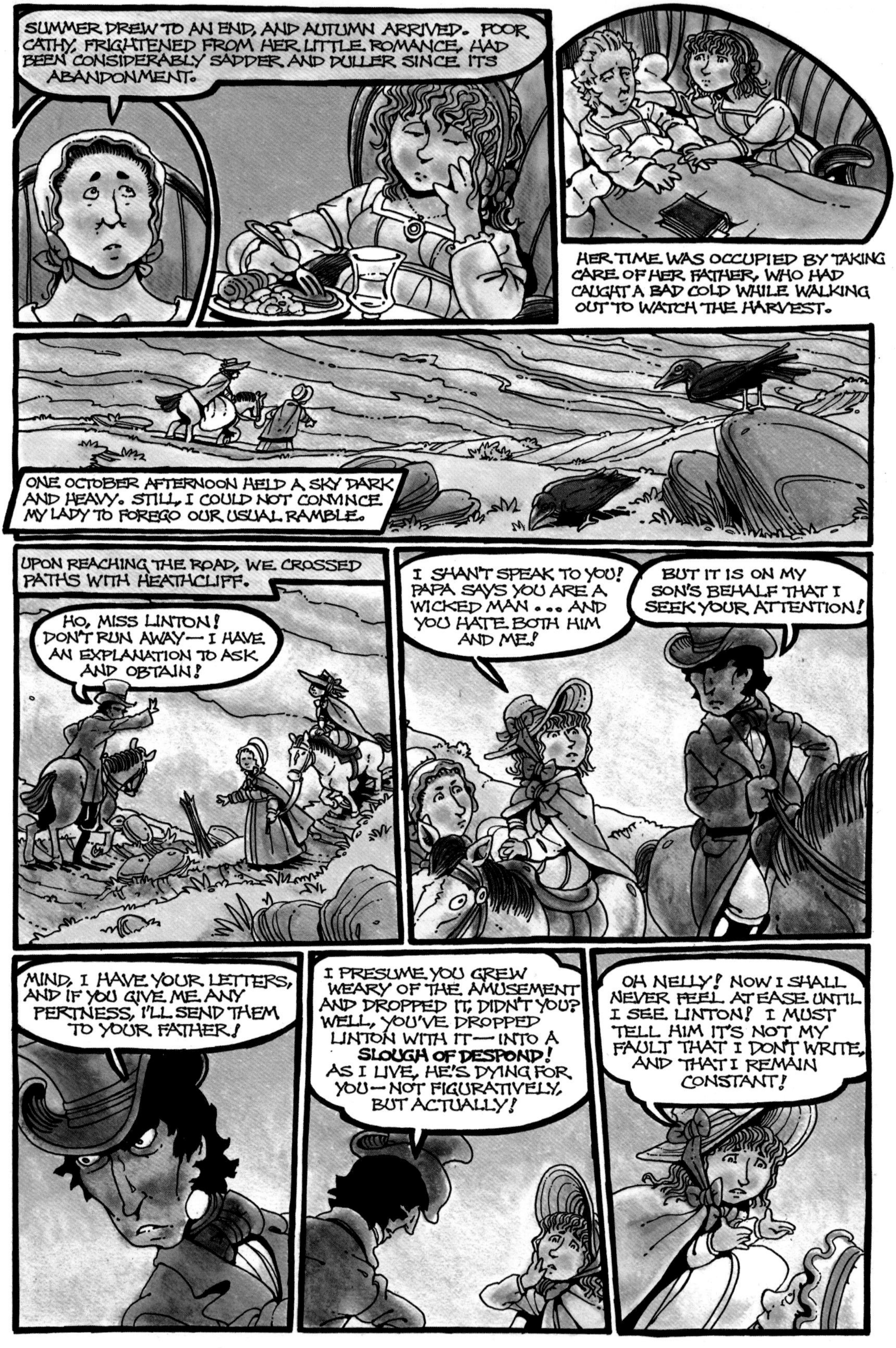
SUMMER DREW TO AN END, AND AUTUMN ARRIVED. POOR CATHY, FRIGHTENED FROM HER LITTLE ROMANCE, HAD BEEN CONSIDERABLY SADDER AND DULLER SINCE ITS ABANDONMENT.
HER TIME WAS OCCUPIED BY TAKING CARE OF HER FATHER, WHO HAD CAUGHT A BAD COLD WHILE WALKING OUT TO WATCH THE HARVEST.
ONE OCTOBER AFTERNOON HELD A SKY DARK AND HEAVY. STILL, I COULD NOT CONVINCE MY LADY TO FOREGO OUR USUAL RAMBLE.
UPON REACHING THE ROAD, WE CROSSED PATHS WITH HEATHCLIFF.
HO, MISS LINTON! DON'T RUN AWAY— I HAVE AN EXPLANATION TO ASK AND OBTAIN!
I SHAN'T SPEAK TO YOU! PAPA SAYS YOU ARE A WICKED MAN ... AND YOU HATE BOTH HIM AND ME!
BUT IT IS ON MY SON'S BEHALF THAT I SEEK YOUR ATTENTION!
MIND, I HAVE YOUR LETTERS, AND IF YOU GIVE ME ANY PERTNESS, I'LL SEND THEM TO YOUR FATHER!
I PRESUME YOU GREW WEARY OF THE AMUSEMENT AND DROPPED IT, DIDN'T YOU? WELL, YOU'VE DROPPED LINTON WITH IT— INTO A SLOUGH OF DESPOND! AS I LIVE, HE'S DYING FOR YOU— NOT FIGURATIVELY, BUT ACTUALLY!
OH NELLY! NOW I SHALL NEVER FEEL AT EASE UNTIL I SEE LINTON! I MUST TELL HIM IT'S NOT MY FAULT THAT I DON'T WRITE, AND THAT I REMAIN CONSTANT!

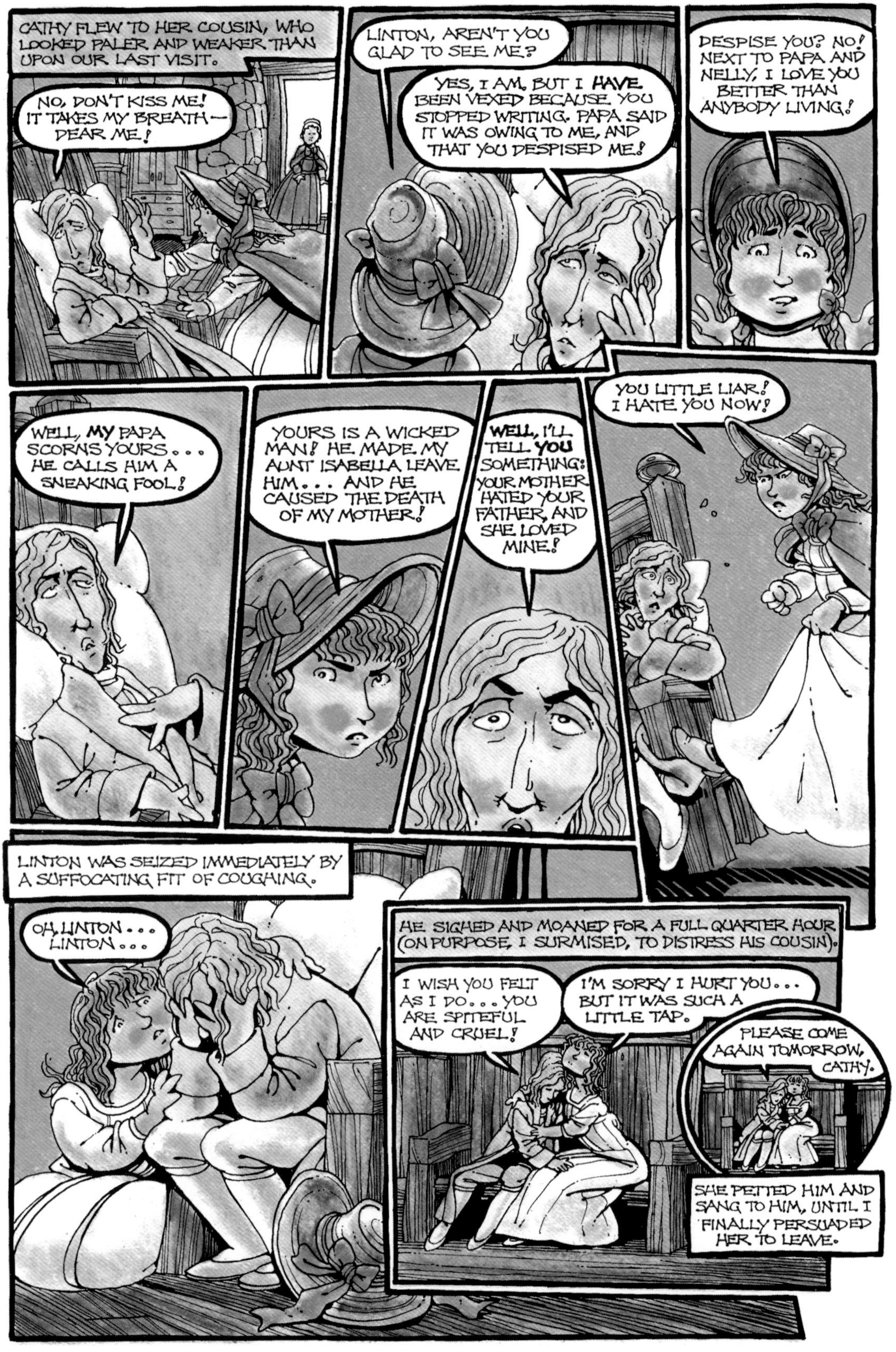
CATHY FLEW TO HER COUSIN, WHO LOOKED PALER AND WEAKER THAN UPON OUR LAST VISIT.
NO, DON'T KISS ME! IT TAKES MY BREATH— DEAR ME!
LINTON, AREN'T YOU GLAD TO SEE ME?
YES, I AM, BUT I HAVE BEEN VEXED BECAUSE YOU STOPPED WRITING. PAPA SAID IT WAS OWING TO ME, AND THAT YOU DESPISED ME!
DESPISE YOU? NO! NEXT TO PAPA AND NELLY, I LOVE YOU BETTER THAN ANYBODY LIVING!
WELL, MY PAPA SCORNS YOURS . . . HE CALLS HIM A SNEAKING FOOL!
YOURS IS A WICKED MAN! HE MADE MY AUNT ISABELLA LEAVE HIM . . . AND HE CAUSED THE DEATH OF MY MOTHER!
WELL, I'LL TELL YOU SOMETHING: YOUR MOTHER HATED YOUR FATHER, AND SHE LOVED MINE!
YOU LITTLE LIAR! I HATE YOU NOW!
LINTON WAS SEIZED IMMEDIATELY BY A SUFFOCATING FIT OF COUGHING.
OH, LINTON . . . LINTON . . .
HE SIGHED AND MOANED FOR A FULL QUARTER HOUR (ON PURPOSE, I SURMISED, TO DISTRESS HIS COUSIN).
I WISH YOU FELT AS I DO . . . YOU ARE SPITEFUL AND CRUEL!
I'M SORRY I HURT YOU . . . BUT IT WAS SUCH A LITTLE TAP.
PLEASE COME AGAIN TOMORROW, CATHY.
SHE PETTED HIM AND SANG TO HIM, UNTIL I FINALLY PERSUADED HER TO LEAVE.

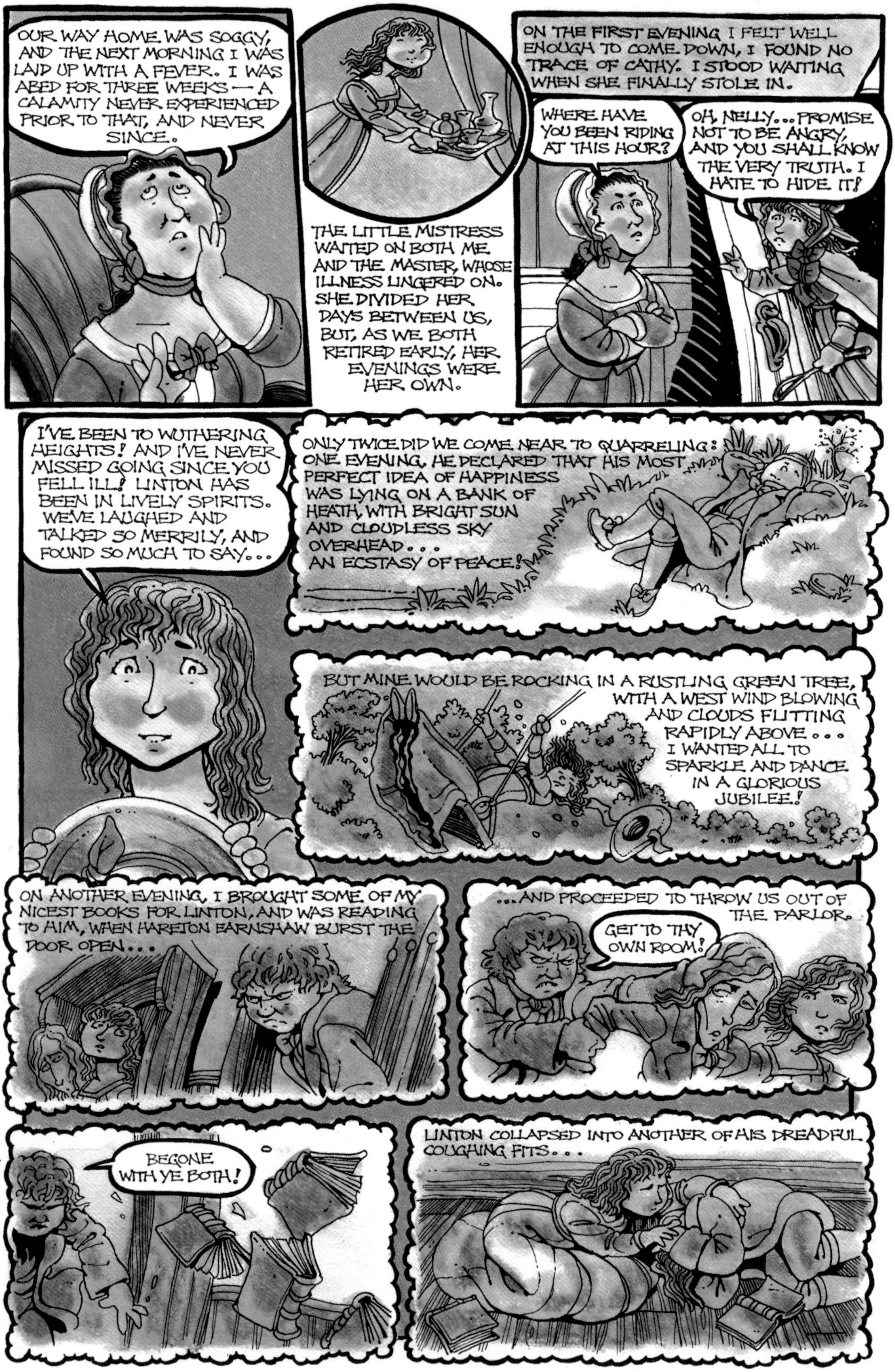
OUR WAY HOME WAS SOGGY, AND THE NEXT MORNING I WAS LAID UP WITH A FEVER. I WAS ABED FOR THREE WEEKS — A CALAMITY NEVER EXPERIENCED PRIOR TO THAT, AND NEVER SINCE.
THE LITTLE MISTRESS WAITED ON BOTH ME AND THE MASTER, WHOSE ILLNESS LINGERED ON. SHE DIVIDED HER DAYS BETWEEN US, BUT, AS WE BOTH RETIRED EARLY, HER EVENINGS WERE HER OWN.
ON THE FIRST EVENING I FELT WELL ENOUGH TO COME DOWN, I FOUND NO TRACE OF CATHY. I STOOD WAITING WHEN SHE FINALLY STOLE IN.
WHERE HAVE YOU BEEN RIDING AT THIS HOUR?
OH, NELLY... PROMISE NOT TO BE ANGRY, AND YOU SHALL KNOW THE VERY TRUTH. I HATE TO HIDE IT!
I'VE BEEN TO WUTHERING HEIGHTS! AND I'VE NEVER MISSED GOING SINCE YOU FELL ILL! LINTON HAS BEEN IN LIVELY SPIRITS. WE'VE LAUGHED AND TALKED SO MERRILY, AND FOUND SO MUCH TO SAY...
ONLY TWICE DID WE COME NEAR TO QUARRELING: ONE EVENING, HE DECLARED THAT HIS MOST PERFECT IDEA OF HAPPINESS WAS LYING ON A BANK OF HEATH, WITH BRIGHT SUN AND CLOUDLESS SKY OVERHEAD... AN ECSTASY OF PEACE!
BUT MINE WOULD BE ROCKING IN A RUSTLING GREEN TREE, WITH A WEST WIND BLOWING AND CLOUDS FLITTING RAPIDLY ABOVE... I WANTED ALL TO SPARKLE AND DANCE IN A GLORIOUS JUBILEE!
ON ANOTHER EVENING, I BROUGHT SOME OF MY NICEST BOOKS FOR LINTON, AND WAS READING TO HIM, WHEN HARETON EARNSHAW BURST THE DOOR OPEN...
...AND PROCEEDED TO THROW US OUT OF THE PARLOR.
GET TO THY OWN ROOM!
BEGONE WITH YE BOTH!
LINTON COLLAPSED INTO ANOTHER OF HIS DREADFUL COUGHING FITS...

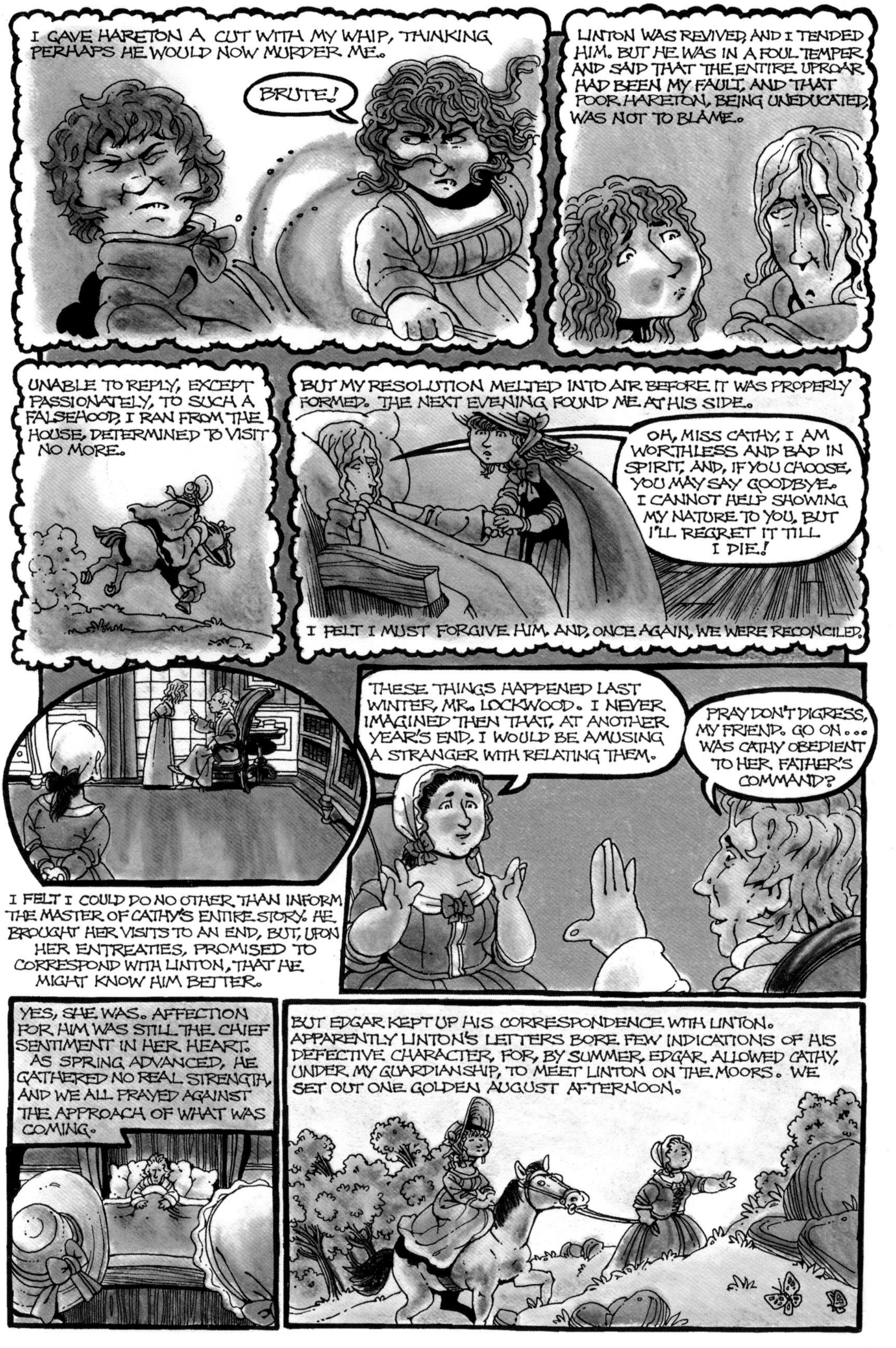
I GAVE HARETON A CUT WITH MY WHIP, THINKING PERHAPS HE WOULD NOW MURDER ME.
BRUTE!
LINTON WAS REVIVED, AND I TENDED HIM. BUT HE WAS IN A FOUL TEMPER AND SAID THAT THE ENTIRE UPROAR HAD BEEN MY FAULT, AND THAT POOR HARETON, BEING UNEDUCATED, WAS NOT TO BLAME.
UNABLE TO REPLY, EXCEPT PASSIONATELY, TO SUCH A FALSEHOOD, I RAN FROM THE HOUSE, DETERMINED TO VISIT NO MORE.
BUT MY RESOLUTION MELTED INTO AIR BEFORE IT WAS PROPERLY FORMED. THE NEXT EVENING FOUND ME AT HIS SIDE.
OH, MISS CATHY, I AM WORTHLESS AND BAD IN SPIRIT, AND, IF YOU CHOOSE, YOU MAY SAY GOODBYE. I CANNOT HELP SHOWING MY NATURE TO YOU, BUT I'LL REGRET IT TILL I DIE!
I FELT I MUST FORGIVE HIM, AND, ONCE AGAIN, WE WERE RECONCILED.
I FELT I COULD DO NO OTHER THAN INFORM THE MASTER OF CATHY'S ENTIRE STORY. HE BROUGHT HER VISITS TO AN END, BUT, UPON HER ENTREATIES, PROMISED TO CORRESPOND WITH LINTON, THAT HE MIGHT KNOW HIM BETTER.
THESE THINGS HAPPENED LAST WINTER, MR. LOCKWOOD. I NEVER IMAGINED THEN THAT, AT ANOTHER YEAR'S END, I WOULD BE AMUSING A STRANGER WITH RELATING THEM.
PRAY DON'T DIGRESS, MY FRIEND. GO ON... WAS CATHY OBEDIENT TO HER FATHER'S COMMAND?
YES, SHE WAS. AFFECTION FOR HIM WAS STILL THE CHIEF SENTIMENT IN HER HEART. AS SPRING ADVANCED, HE GATHERED NO REAL STRENGTH, AND WE ALL PRAYED AGAINST THE APPROACH OF WHAT WAS COMING.
BUT EDGAR KEPT UP HIS CORRESPONDENCE WITH LINTON. APPARENTLY LINTON'S LETTERS BORE FEW INDICATIONS OF HIS DEFECTIVE CHARACTER, FOR, BY SUMMER, EDGAR ALLOWED CATHY, UNDER MY GUARDIANSHIP, TO MEET LINTON ON THE MOORS. WE SET OUT ONE GOLDEN AUGUST AFTERNOON.

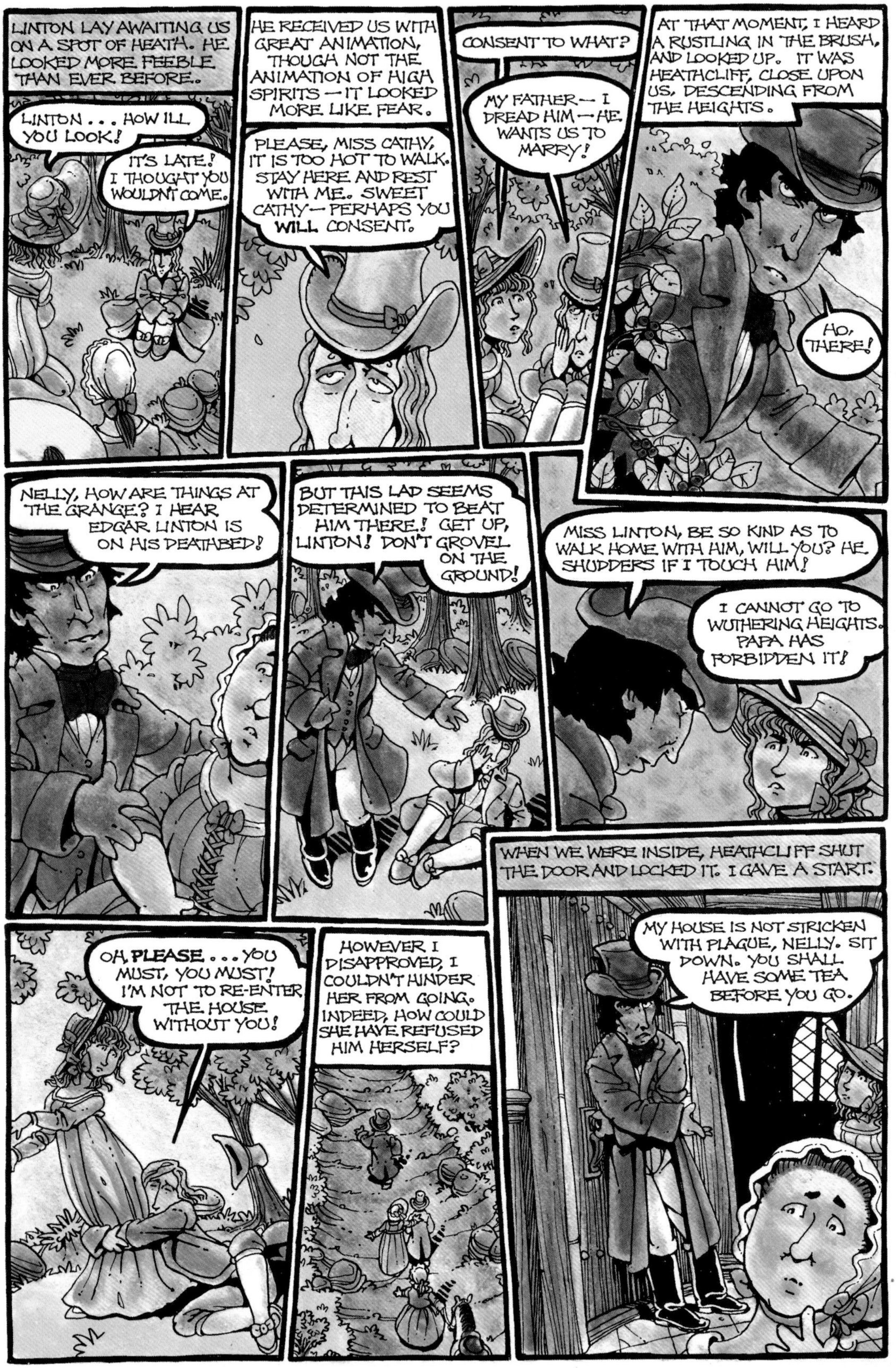
LINTON LAY AWAITING US ON A SPOT OF HEATH. HE LOOKED MORE FEEBLE THAN EVER BEFORE.
LINTON . . . HOW ILL YOU LOOK!
IT'S LATE! I THOUGHT YOU WOULDN'T COME.
HE RECEIVED US WITH GREAT ANIMATION, THOUGH NOT THE ANIMATION OF HIGH SPIRITS — IT LOOKED MORE LIKE FEAR.
PLEASE, MISS CATHY, IT IS TOO HOT TO WALK. STAY HERE AND REST WITH ME. SWEET CATHY— PERHAPS YOU **WILL** CONSENT.
CONSENT TO WHAT?
MY FATHER— I DREAD HIM —HE WANTS US TO MARRY!
AT THAT MOMENT, I HEARD A RUSTLING IN THE BRUSH, AND LOOKED UP. IT WAS HEATHCLIFF, CLOSE UPON US, DESCENDING FROM THE HEIGHTS.
HO, THERE!
NELLY, HOW ARE THINGS AT THE GRANGE? I HEAR EDGAR LINTON IS ON HIS DEATHBED!
BUT THIS LAD SEEMS DETERMINED TO BEAT HIM THERE! GET UP, LINTON! DON'T GROVEL ON THE GROUND!
MISS LINTON, BE SO KIND AS TO WALK HOME WITH HIM, WILL YOU? HE SHUDDERS IF I TOUCH HIM!
I CANNOT GO TO WUTHERING HEIGHTS. PAPA HAS FORBIDDEN IT!
OH, **PLEASE** . . . YOU MUST, YOU MUST! I'M NOT TO RE-ENTER THE HOUSE WITHOUT YOU!
HOWEVER I DISAPPROVED, I COULDN'T HINDER HER FROM GOING. INDEED, HOW COULD SHE HAVE REFUSED HIM HERSELF?
WHEN WE WERE INSIDE, HEATHCLIFF SHUT THE DOOR AND LOCKED IT. I GAVE A START.
MY HOUSE IS NOT STRICKEN WITH PLAGUE, NELLY. SIT DOWN. YOU SHALL HAVE SOME TEA BEFORE YOU GO.

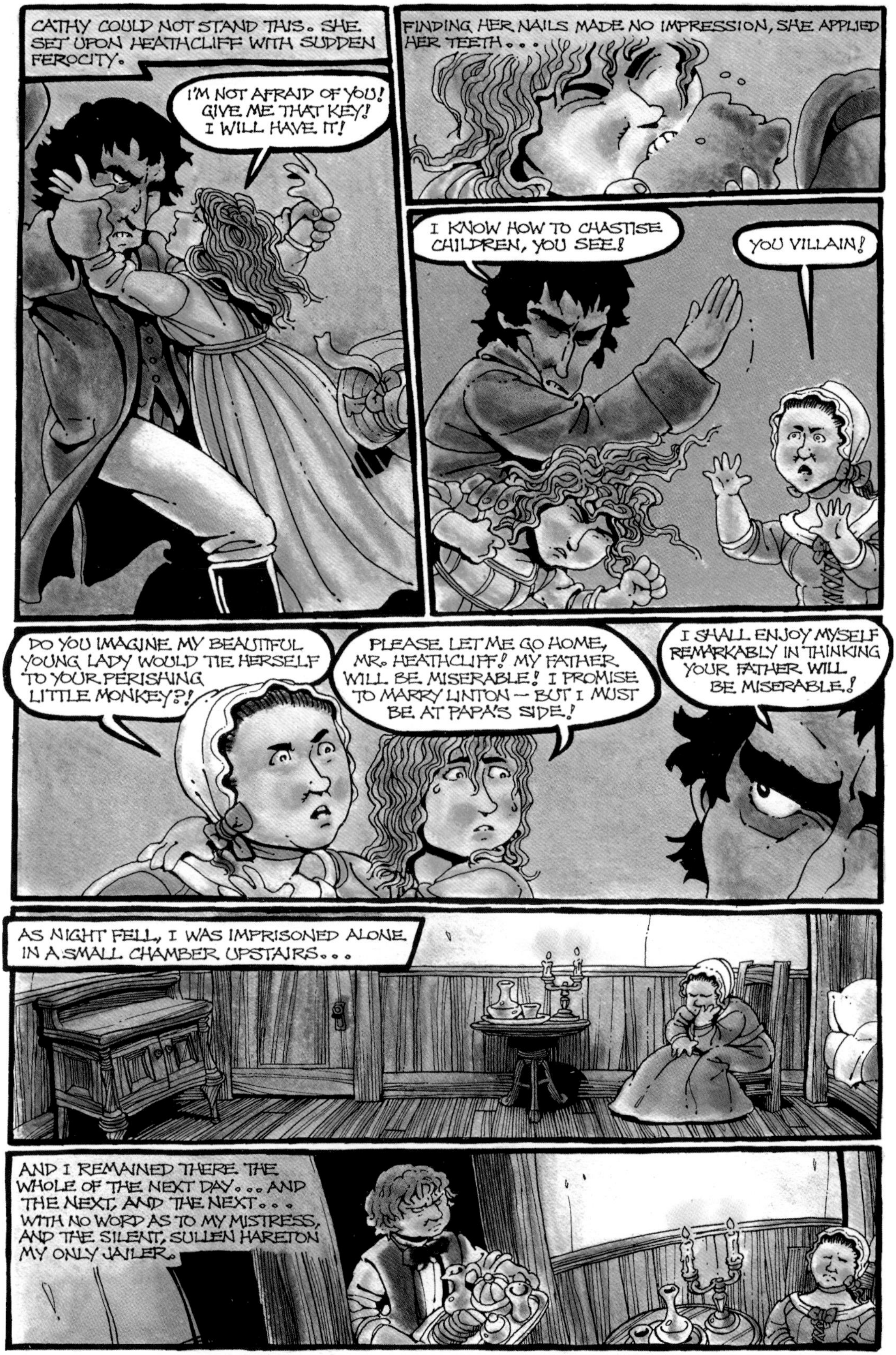

CATHY COULD NOT STAND THIS. SHE SET UPON HEATHCLIFF WITH SUDDEN FEROCITY.
I'M NOT AFRAID OF YOU! GIVE ME THAT KEY! I WILL HAVE IT!
FINDING HER NAILS MADE NO IMPRESSION, SHE APPLIED HER TEETH...
I KNOW HOW TO CHASTISE CHILDREN, YOU SEE!
YOU VILLAIN!
DO YOU IMAGINE MY BEAUTIFUL YOUNG LADY WOULD TIE HERSELF TO YOUR PERISHING LITTLE MONKEY?!
PLEASE LET ME GO HOME, MR. HEATHCLIFF! MY FATHER WILL BE MISERABLE! I PROMISE TO MARRY LINTON — BUT I MUST BE AT PAPA'S SIDE!
I SHALL ENJOY MYSELF REMARKABLY IN THINKING YOUR FATHER WILL BE MISERABLE!
AS NIGHT FELL, I WAS IMPRISONED ALONE IN A SMALL CHAMBER UPSTAIRS...
AND I REMAINED THERE THE WHOLE OF THE NEXT DAY... AND THE NEXT, AND THE NEXT... WITH NO WORD AS TO MY MISTRESS, AND THE SILENT, SULLEN HARETON MY ONLY JAILER.

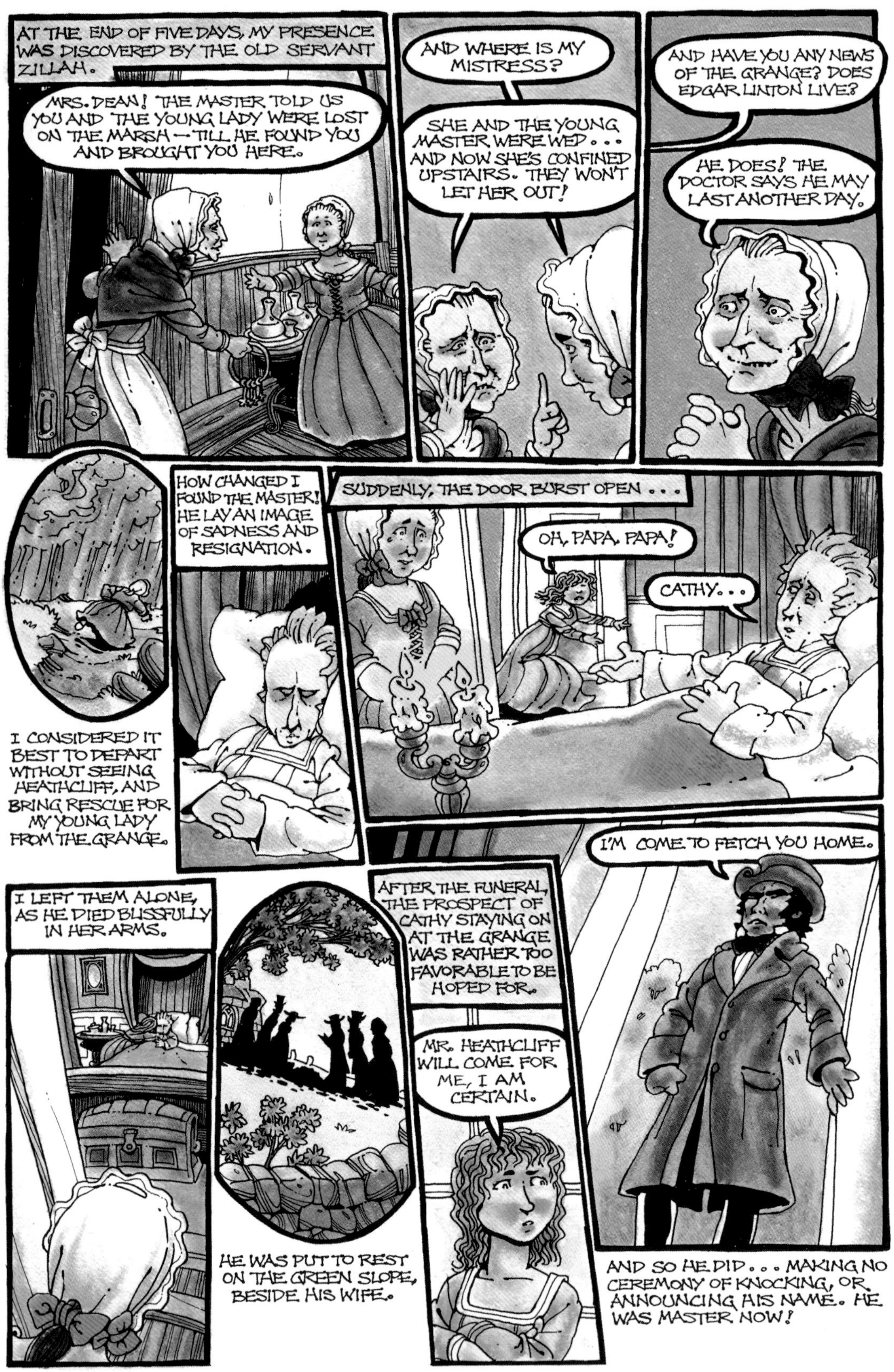
AT THE END OF FIVE DAYS, MY PRESENCE WAS DISCOVERED BY THE OLD SERVANT ZILLAH.
MRS. DEAN! THE MASTER TOLD US YOU AND THE YOUNG LADY WERE LOST ON THE MARSH -- TILL HE FOUND YOU AND BROUGHT YOU HERE.
AND WHERE IS MY MISTRESS?
SHE AND THE YOUNG MASTER WERE WED . . . AND NOW SHE'S CONFINED UPSTAIRS. THEY WON'T LET HER OUT!
AND HAVE YOU ANY NEWS OF THE GRANGE? DOES EDGAR LINTON LIVE?
HE DOES! THE DOCTOR SAYS HE MAY LAST ANOTHER DAY.
I CONSIDERED IT BEST TO DEPART WITHOUT SEEING HEATHCLIFF, AND BRING RESCUE FOR MY YOUNG LADY FROM THE GRANGE.
HOW CHANGED I FOUND THE MASTER! HE LAY AN IMAGE OF SADNESS AND RESIGNATION.
SUDDENLY, THE DOOR BURST OPEN . . .
OH, PAPA, PAPA!
CATHY. . .
I LEFT THEM ALONE, AS HE DIED BLISSFULLY IN HER ARMS.
HE WAS PUT TO REST ON THE GREEN SLOPE, BESIDE HIS WIFE.
AFTER THE FUNERAL, THE PROSPECT OF CATHY STAYING ON AT THE GRANGE WAS RATHER TOO FAVORABLE TO BE HOPED FOR.
MR. HEATHCLIFF WILL COME FOR ME, I AM CERTAIN.
I'M COME TO FETCH YOU HOME.
AND SO HE DID . . . MAKING NO CEREMONY OF KNOCKING, OR ANNOUNCING HIS NAME. HE WAS MASTER NOW!

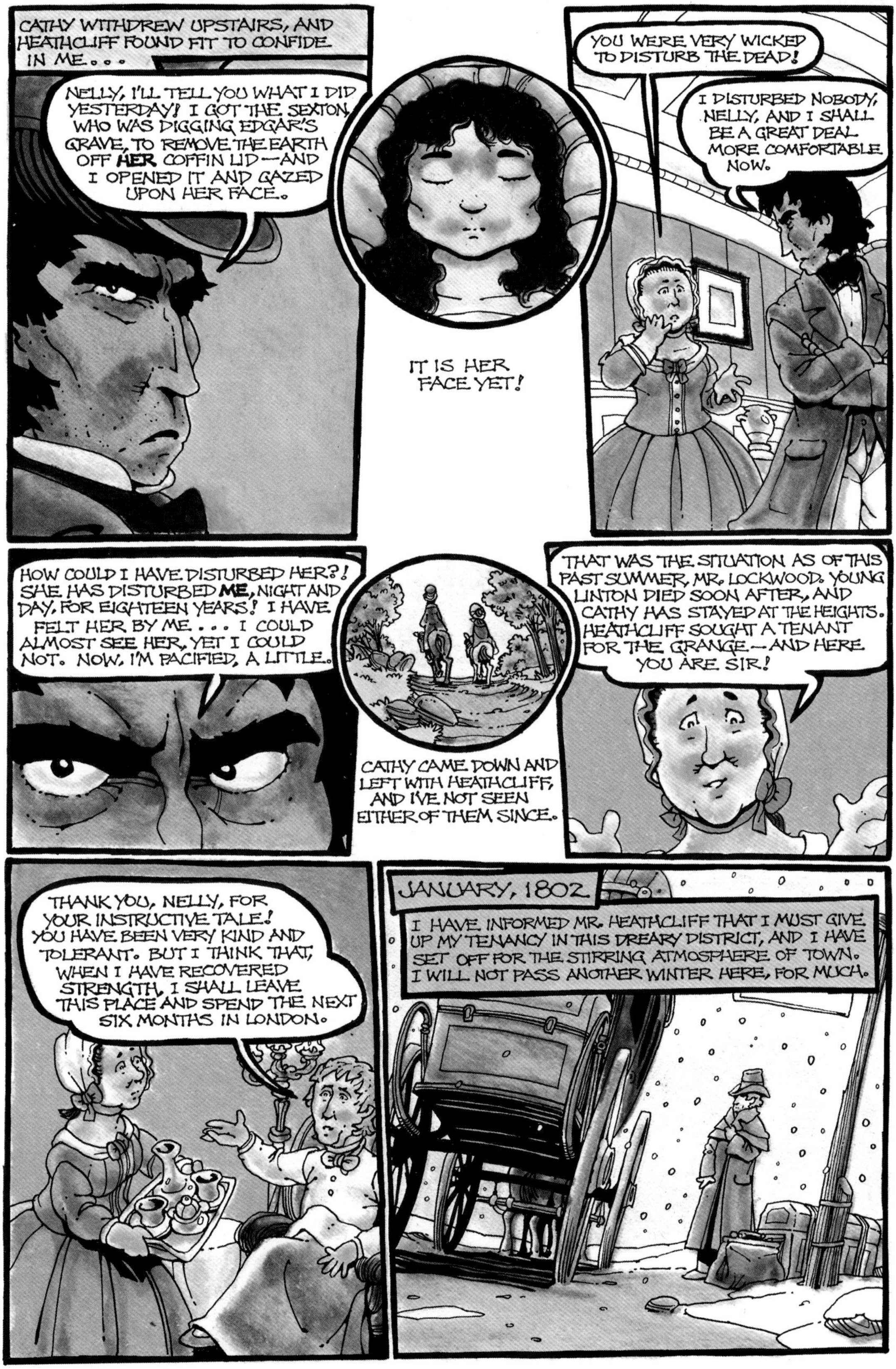
CATHY WITHDREW UPSTAIRS, AND HEATHCLIFF FOUND FIT TO CONFIDE IN ME...
NELLY, I'LL TELL YOU WHAT I DID YESTERDAY! I GOT THE SEXTON, WHO WAS DIGGING EDGAR'S GRAVE, TO REMOVE THE EARTH OFF **HER** COFFIN LID—AND I OPENED IT AND GAZED UPON HER FACE.
IT IS HER FACE YET!
YOU WERE VERY WICKED TO DISTURB THE DEAD!
I DISTURBED NOBODY, NELLY, AND I SHALL BE A GREAT DEAL MORE COMFORTABLE NOW.
HOW COULD I HAVE DISTURBED HER?! SHE HAS DISTURBED **ME**, NIGHT AND DAY, FOR EIGHTEEN YEARS! I HAVE FELT HER BY ME... I COULD ALMOST SEE HER, YET I COULD NOT. NOW, I'M PACIFIED, A LITTLE.
CATHY CAME DOWN AND LEFT WITH HEATHCLIFF, AND I'VE NOT SEEN EITHER OF THEM SINCE.
THAT WAS THE SITUATION AS OF THIS PAST SUMMER, MR. LOCKWOOD. YOUNG LINTON DIED SOON AFTER, AND CATHY HAS STAYED AT THE HEIGHTS. HEATHCLIFF SOUGHT A TENANT FOR THE GRANGE—AND HERE YOU ARE SIR!
THANK YOU, NELLY, FOR YOUR INSTRUCTIVE TALE! YOU HAVE BEEN VERY KIND AND TOLERANT. BUT I THINK THAT, WHEN I HAVE RECOVERED STRENGTH, I SHALL LEAVE THIS PLACE AND SPEND THE NEXT SIX MONTHS IN LONDON.
JANUARY, 1802
I HAVE INFORMED MR. HEATHCLIFF THAT I MUST GIVE UP MY TENANCY IN THIS DREARY DISTRICT, AND I HAVE SET OFF FOR THE STIRRING ATMOSPHERE OF TOWN. I WILL NOT PASS ANOTHER WINTER HERE, FOR MUCH.

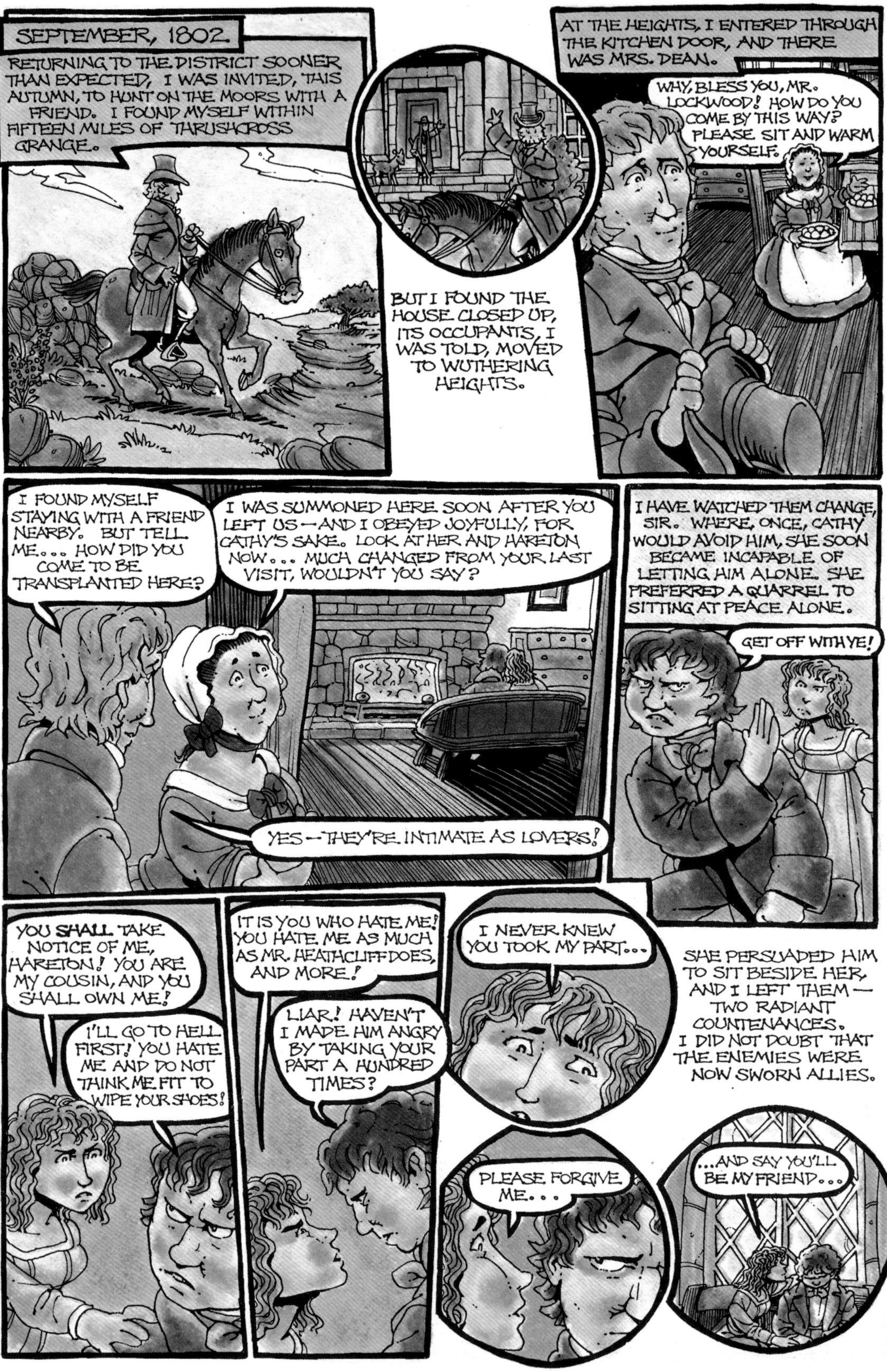
SEPTEMBER, 1802.
RETURNING TO THE DISTRICT SOONER THAN EXPECTED, I WAS INVITED, THIS AUTUMN, TO HUNT ON THE MOORS WITH A FRIEND. I FOUND MYSELF WITHIN FIFTEEN MILES OF THRUSHCROSS GRANGE.
BUT I FOUND THE HOUSE CLOSED UP, ITS OCCUPANTS, I WAS TOLD, MOVED TO WUTHERING HEIGHTS.
AT THE HEIGHTS, I ENTERED THROUGH THE KITCHEN DOOR, AND THERE WAS MRS. DEAN.
WHY, BLESS YOU, MR. LOCKWOOD! HOW DO YOU COME BY THIS WAY? PLEASE SIT AND WARM YOURSELF.
I FOUND MYSELF STAYING WITH A FRIEND NEARBY. BUT TELL ME... HOW DID YOU COME TO BE TRANSPLANTED HERE?
I WAS SUMMONED HERE SOON AFTER YOU LEFT US—AND I OBEYED JOYFULLY, FOR CATHY'S SAKE. LOOK AT HER AND HARETON NOW... MUCH CHANGED FROM YOUR LAST VISIT, WOULDN'T YOU SAY?
YES—THEY'RE INTIMATE AS LOVERS!
I HAVE WATCHED THEM CHANGE, SIR. WHERE, ONCE, CATHY WOULD AVOID HIM, SHE SOON BECAME INCAPABLE OF LETTING HIM ALONE. SHE PREFERRED A QUARREL TO SITTING AT PEACE ALONE.
GET OFF WITH YE!
YOU SHALL TAKE NOTICE OF ME, HARETON! YOU ARE MY COUSIN, AND YOU SHALL OWN ME!
I'LL GO TO HELL FIRST! YOU HATE ME AND DO NOT THINK ME FIT TO WIPE YOUR SHOES!
IT IS YOU WHO HATE ME! YOU HATE ME AS MUCH AS MR. HEATHCLIFF DOES, AND MORE!
LIAR! HAVEN'T I MADE HIM ANGRY BY TAKING YOUR PART A HUNDRED TIMES?
I NEVER KNEW YOU TOOK MY PART...
PLEASE FORGIVE ME...
...AND SAY YOU'LL BE MY FRIEND...
SHE PERSUADED HIM TO SIT BESIDE HER, AND I LEFT THEM—TWO RADIANT COUNTENANCES. I DID NOT DOUBT THAT THE ENEMIES WERE NOW SWORN ALLIES.

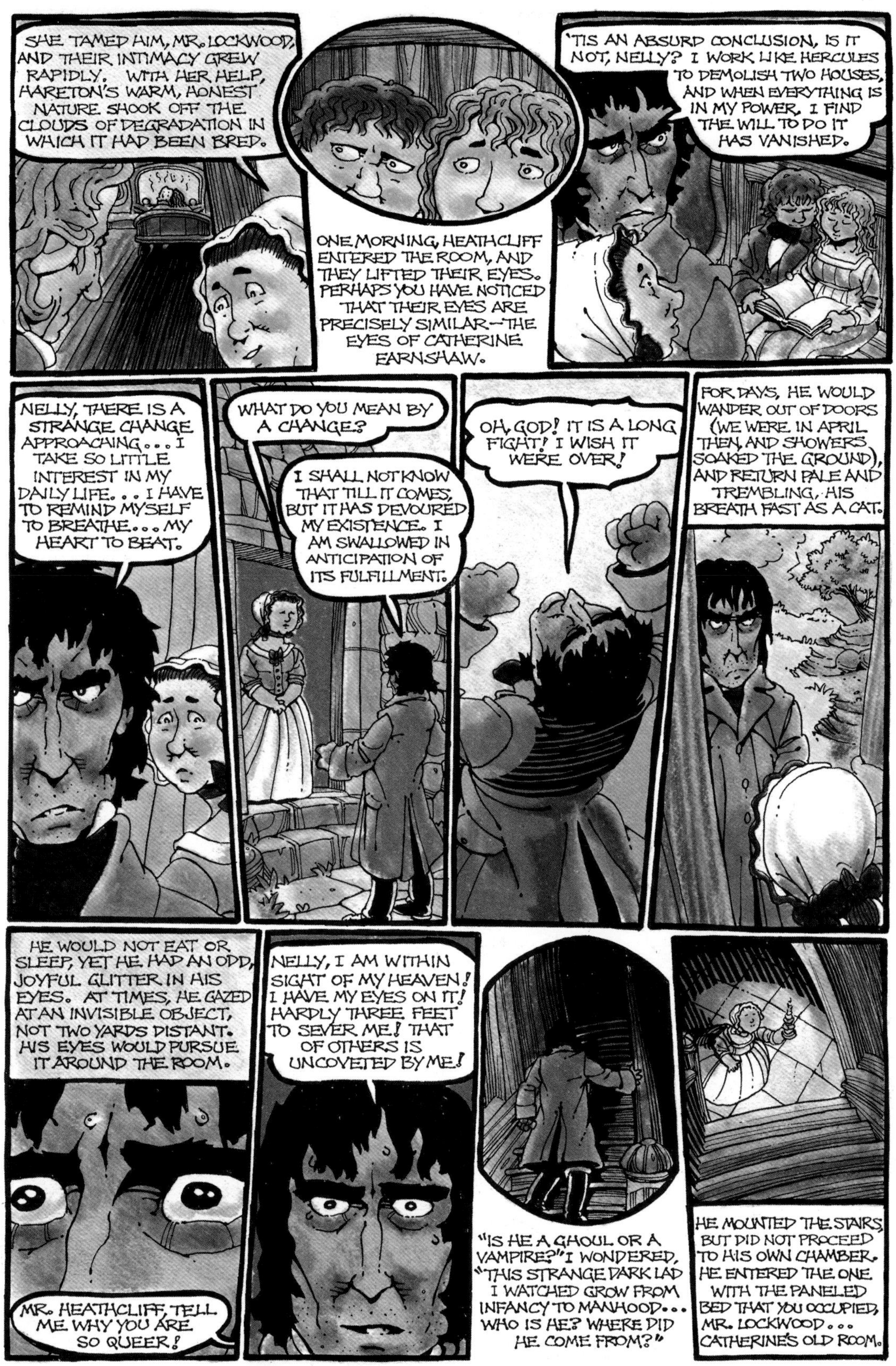
SHE TAMED HIM, MR. LOCKWOOD, AND THEIR INTIMACY GREW RAPIDLY. WITH HER HELP, HARETON'S WARM, HONEST NATURE SHOOK OFF THE CLOUDS OF DEGRADATION IN WHICH IT HAD BEEN BRED.
ONE MORNING, HEATHCLIFF ENTERED THE ROOM, AND THEY LIFTED THEIR EYES. PERHAPS YOU HAVE NOTICED THAT THEIR EYES ARE PRECISELY SIMILAR—THE EYES OF CATHERINE EARNSHAW.
'TIS AN ABSURD CONCLUSION, IS IT NOT, NELLY? I WORK LIKE HERCULES TO DEMOLISH TWO HOUSES, AND WHEN EVERYTHING IS IN MY POWER, I FIND THE WILL TO DO IT HAS VANISHED.
NELLY, THERE IS A STRANGE CHANGE APPROACHING... I TAKE SO LITTLE INTEREST IN MY DAILY LIFE... I HAVE TO REMIND MYSELF TO BREATHE... MY HEART TO BEAT.
WHAT DO YOU MEAN BY A CHANGE?
I SHALL NOT KNOW THAT TILL IT COMES, BUT IT HAS DEVOURED MY EXISTENCE. I AM SWALLOWED IN ANTICIPATION OF ITS FULFILLMENT.
OH, GOD! IT IS A LONG FIGHT! I WISH IT WERE OVER!
FOR DAYS, HE WOULD WANDER OUT OF DOORS (WE WERE IN APRIL THEN, AND SHOWERS SOAKED THE GROUND), AND RETURN PALE AND TREMBLING, HIS BREATH FAST AS A CAT.
HE WOULD NOT EAT OR SLEEP, YET HE HAD AN ODD, JOYFUL GLITTER IN HIS EYES. AT TIMES, HE GAZED AT AN INVISIBLE OBJECT, NOT TWO YARDS DISTANT. HIS EYES WOULD PURSUE IT AROUND THE ROOM.
MR. HEATHCLIFF, TELL ME WHY YOU ARE SO QUEER!
NELLY, I AM WITHIN SIGHT OF MY HEAVEN! I HAVE MY EYES ON IT! HARDLY THREE FEET TO SEVER ME! THAT OF OTHERS IS UNCOVETED BY ME!
"IS HE A GHOUL OR A VAMPIRE?" I WONDERED, "THIS STRANGE DARK LAD I WATCHED GROW FROM INFANCY TO MANHOOD... WHO IS HE? WHERE DID HE COME FROM?"
HE MOUNTED THE STAIRS, BUT DID NOT PROCEED TO HIS OWN CHAMBER. HE ENTERED THE ONE WITH THE PANELED BED THAT YOU OCCUPIED, MR. LOCKWOOD... CATHERINE'S OLD ROOM.

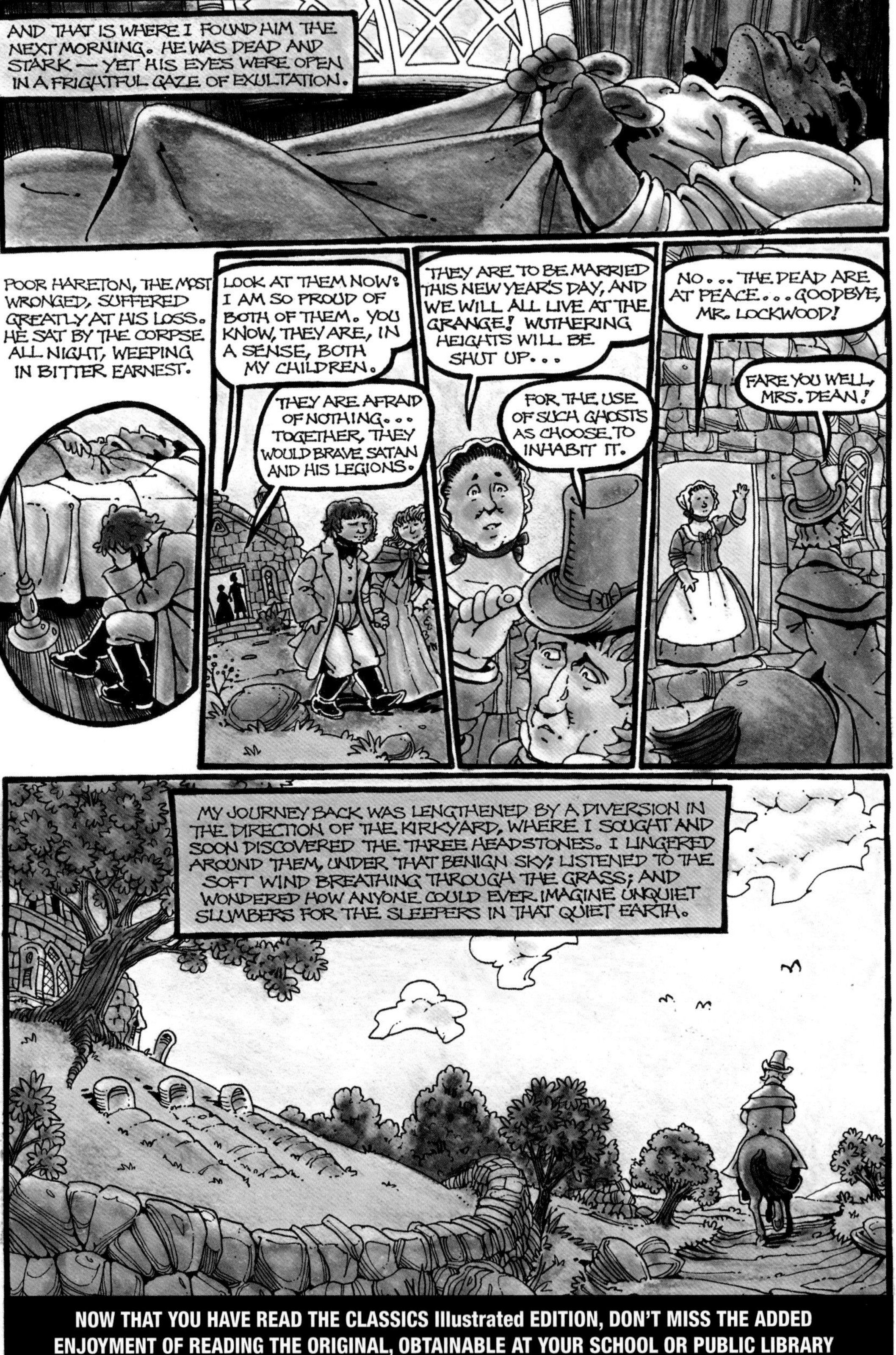
AND THAT IS WHERE I FOUND HIM THE NEXT MORNING. HE WAS DEAD AND STARK — YET HIS EYES WERE OPEN IN A FRIGHTFUL GAZE OF EXULTATION.
POOR HARETON, THE MOST WRONGED, SUFFERED GREATLY AT HIS LOSS. HE SAT BY THE CORPSE ALL NIGHT, WEEPING IN BITTER EARNEST.
LOOK AT THEM NOW: I AM SO PROUD OF BOTH OF THEM. YOU KNOW, THEY ARE, IN A SENSE, BOTH MY CHILDREN.
THEY ARE AFRAID OF NOTHING... TOGETHER, THEY WOULD BRAVE SATAN AND HIS LEGIONS.
THEY ARE TO BE MARRIED THIS NEW YEAR'S DAY, AND WE WILL ALL LIVE AT THE GRANGE! WUTHERING HEIGHTS WILL BE SHUT UP...
FOR THE USE OF SUCH GHOSTS AS CHOOSE TO INHABIT IT.
NO... THE DEAD ARE AT PEACE... GOODBYE, MR. LOCKWOOD!
FARE YOU WELL, MRS. DEAN!
MY JOURNEY BACK WAS LENGTHENED BY A DIVERSION IN THE DIRECTION OF THE KIRKYARD, WHERE I SOUGHT AND SOON DISCOVERED THE THREE HEADSTONES. I LINGERED AROUND THEM, UNDER THAT BENIGN SKY; LISTENED TO THE SOFT WIND BREATHING THROUGH THE GRASS; AND WONDERED HOW ANYONE COULD EVER IMAGINE UNQUIET SLUMBERS FOR THE SLEEPERS IN THAT QUIET EARTH.

NOW THAT YOU HAVE READ THE CLASSICS Illustrated EDITION, DON'T MISS THE ADDED ENJOYMENT OF READING THE ORIGINAL, OBTAINABLE AT YOUR SCHOOL OR PUBLIC LIBRARY

WATCH OUT FOR PAPERCUTZ

Welcome to the hopelessly romantic fourteenth edition of the Papercutz CLASSICS ILLUSTRAT-
ED graphic novel series, featuring Rick Geary's impressive comics adaptation of Emily Brontë's
Wuthering Heights. I'm Jim Salicrup, part-time groundskeeper and full-time Editor-in-Chief of
Papercutz, publishers of graphic novels for all ages.

As you may already know, CLASSICS ILLUSTRATED started 70 years ago, in October 1941 to be
precise, as a comicbook aptly called CLASSIC COMICS. It was rechristened CLASSICS ILLUSTRAT-
ED with issue No. 35 in 1947. First Publishing revived CLASSICS ILLUSTRATED in 1990 (the original comicbook series ended in 1971), they changed the format to paperback graphic novels,
printed on slick paper with full-color printing. But they still stayed at 48 pages, and a whole new
generation of comicbook artists and writers had to wrestle with trying to squeeze classic works of
literature into an incredibly limited amount of space. Some volumes worked out wonderfully. For
example, the premiere edition of First Publishing's incarnation of CLASSICS ILLUSTRATED fea-
tured Edgar Allan Poe's *The Raven and Other Poems* as illustrated by Gahan Wilson. The poems
selected weren't that long and were published unabridged, with plenty of room left for the cele-
brated cartoonist's suitably macabre illustrations (that volume was republished in hardcover as
the fourth edition in the current Papercutz series). Plays such as William Shakespeare's *Hamlet* and
Edmond Rostand's *Cyrano de Begerac* didn't seem to suffer much as they were adapted into comics
by Steven Grant and Tom Mandrake, and Peter David and Kyle Baker, respectively (See CLASSICS
ILLUSTRATED #5 and #10). Astoundingly, artist/writer Rick Geary was even able to adapt Charles
Dickens's *Great Expectations* (in CLASSICS ILLUSTRATED #1) in a way that captures the essence
and main plotline quite well. And that brings us to our current edition, adapting Emily Brontë's
Wuthering Heights.

What can we say about the Eisner Award-Winning Rick Geary? He makes these adaptations work
so well, that you'd hardly believe they were based upon such lengthy novels. For more wonderful work by Mr. Geary we strongly suggest his two series from NBM Publishing—*A Treasury of
Victorian Murder* and *A Treasury of XXth Century Murder*. The latest volume of the latter series, "The
Lives of Sacco and Vinzetti," has just been released, and it's highly recommended by yours truly.
Like all Papercutz books, these NBM titles should be available at booksellers (bookstores, comicbook stores, and online booksellers) everywhere.

Regarding adapting novels into 48 pages of comics, you may be asking, well, why didn't they
just use more pages of comics to better adapt the novels? Originally, and for many years to follow, the cost was just too prohibitive. But now, as the world has embraced the graphic novel format, it's now possible. Simply check out CLASSICS ILLUSTRATED DELUXE, our companion
graphic novel series, to find all-new, longer-than-ever comics adaptations of such novels as
Frankenstein, Treasure Island, The Adventures of Tom Sawyer, and more. We're running a special
romantic excerpt in a few pages of the currently available adaptation of "The Three Musketeers"
by Alexandre Dumas, as adapted by Morvan, Duframme, and Rubén. It's in CLASSICS ILLUSTRAT-
ED DELUXE #6, and the adaptation is 191 pages long! Also, take a look at short previews of two
new titles from Papercutz we hope you will love: ERNEST & REBECCA and SYBIL THE BACKPACK
FAIRY. Both new series will premiere in November 2011.

Next up in CLASSICS ILLUSTRATED #15— *The Call of the Wild* by Jack London, adapted by
Charles Dixon and Ricardo Villagran. You don't want to miss it!

We like to hear what you think of CLASSICS ILLUSTRATED! Either email me at salicrup@paper-
cutz.com or send an old-fashioned paper letter to CLASSICS ILLUSTRATED, Papercutz, 40
Exchange Place, Suite 1308, New York, NY 10005.

Thanks, *Jim*

CLASSICS ILLUSTRATED DELUXE
GRAPHIC NOVELS FROM PAPERCUTZ

FULL-COLOR GRAPHIC NOVEL ADAPTATION
CLASSICS Illustrated Deluxe
THE WIND IN THE WILLOWS
By Kenneth Grahame
Adapted by Michel Plessix
"A VISUAL MASTERPIECE.." -NEWSWEEK
PAPERCUTZ

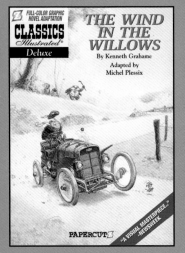

#1 "The Wind In The Willows"

FULL-COLOR GRAPHIC NOVEL ADAPTATION
CLASSICS Illustrated Deluxe
TALES FROM THE BROTHERS GRIMM
Adapted by Mazan, Cecile Chicault, and Philip Petit
PAPERCUTZ

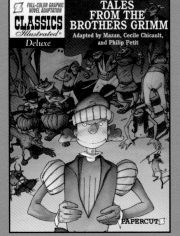

#2 "Tales From The Brothers Grimm"

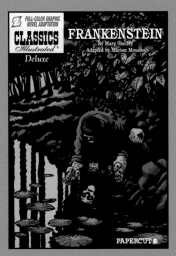

FULL-COLOR GRAPHIC NOVEL ADAPTATION
CLASSICS Illustrated Deluxe
FRANKENSTEIN
By Mary Shelley
Adapted by Marion Mousse
PAPERCUTZ

#3 "Frankenstein"

FULL-COLOR GRAPHIC NOVEL ADAPTATION
CLASSICS Illustrated Deluxe
The Adventures of TOM SAWYER
BY MARK TWAIN
PAPERCUTZ

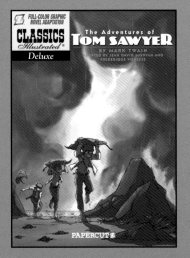

#4 "The Adventures of Tom Sawyer"

FULL-COLOR GRAPHIC NOVEL ADAPTATION
CLASSICS Illustrated Deluxe
TREASURE ISLAND
By Robert Louis Stevenson
Adapted by Chauvel and Simon
PAPERCUTZ

#5 "Treasure Island"

FULL-COLOR GRAPHIC NOVEL ADAPTATION
CLASSICS Illustrated Deluxe
The Three MUSKETEERS
BY ALEXANDRE DUMAS
Adapted by Morvan, Dufranne & Rubén
70th Anniversary Edition
PAPERCUTZ

#6 "The Three Musketeers"

CLASSICS ILLUSTRATED DELUXE graphic novels are available for $13.95 each in paperback and $17.95 in hardcover, except for #6, $16.99 pb., $21.99 hc. Please add $4.00 for postage and handling for the first book, add $1.00 for each additional book. MC, Visa, Amex accepted or make check payable to NBM Publishing. Send to: Papercutz, 40 Exchange Place, Ste. 1308, New York, NY 10005 • 1-800-886-1223

WWW.PAPERCUTZ.COM

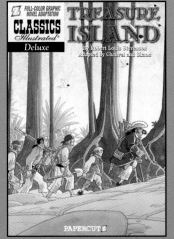

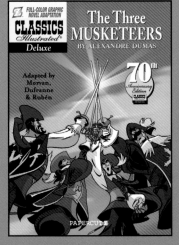

Special preview of ERNEST & REBECCA #1 "My Best Friend is a Germ"

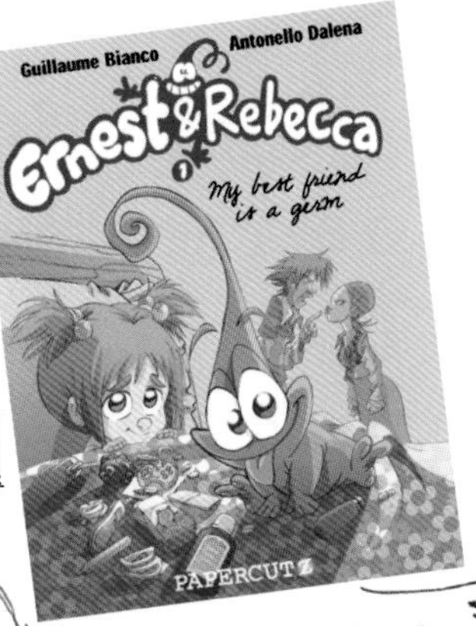
Guillaume Bianco
Antonello Dalena
Ernest & Rebecca
1
My best friend is a germ
PAPERCUTZ

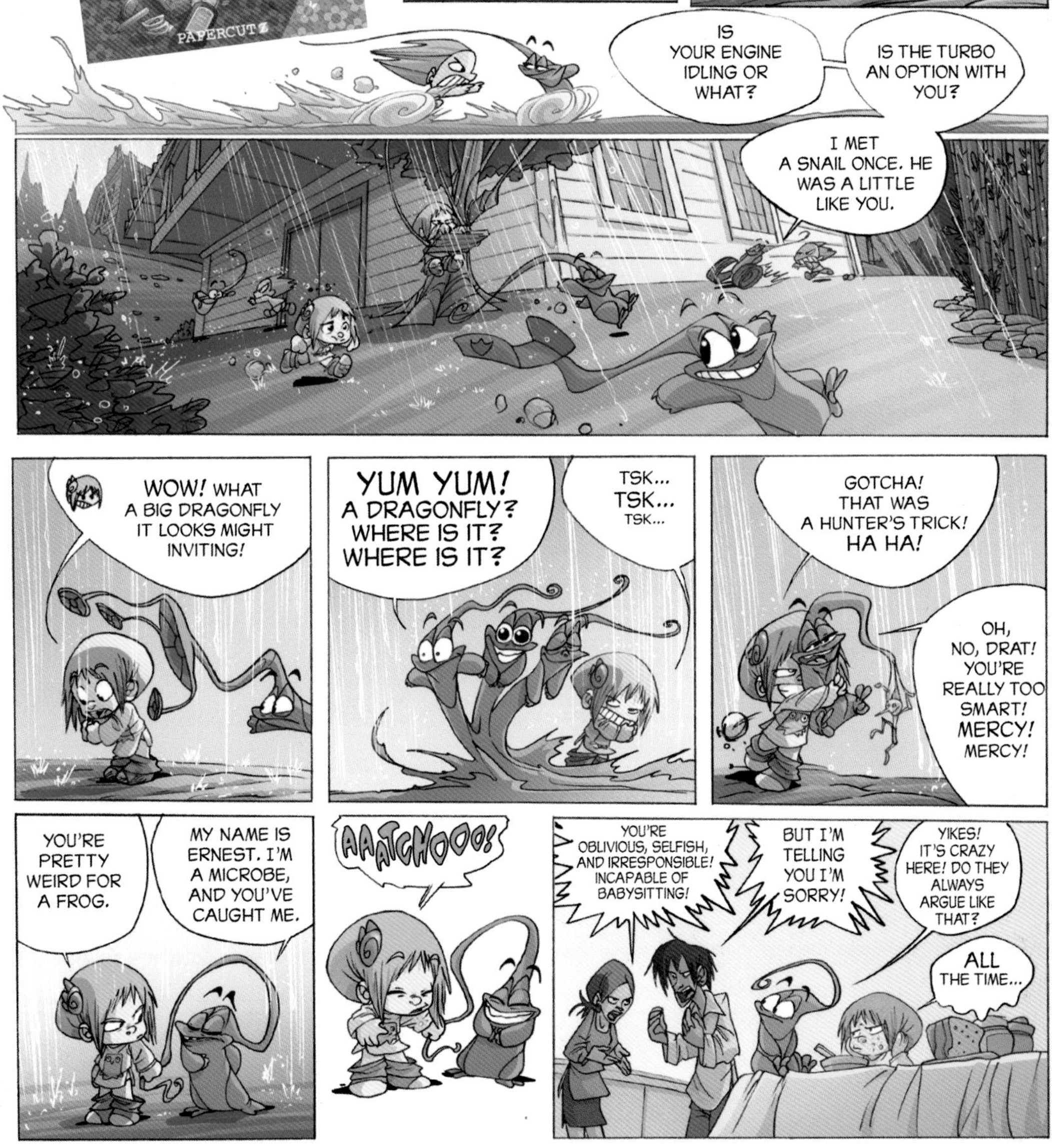
IT SEEMS THAT LITTLE PIGS LOVE MUD BATHS!
DIRTY FROG! YOU WON'T ACT SO PROUD ONCE YOU'RE ON MY PLATE!
IS YOUR ENGINE IDLING OR WHAT?
IS THE TURBO AN OPTION WITH YOU?
I MET A SNAIL ONCE. HE WAS A LITTLE LIKE YOU.
WOW! WHAT A BIG DRAGONFLY IT LOOKS MIGHT INVITING!
YUM YUM! A DRAGONFLY? WHERE IS IT? WHERE IS IT?
TSK... TSK... TSK...
GOTCHA! THAT WAS A HUNTER'S TRICK! HA HA!
OH, NO, DRAT! YOU'RE REALLY TOO SMART! MERCY! MERCY!
YOU'RE PRETTY WEIRD FOR A FROG.
MY NAME IS ERNEST. I'M A MICROBE, AND YOU'VE CAUGHT ME.
AAATCHOOO!
YOU'RE OBLIVIOUS, SELFISH, AND IRRESPONSIBLE! INCAPABLE OF BABYSITTING!
BUT I'M TELLING YOU I'M SORRY!
YIKES! IT'S CRAZY HERE! DO THEY ALWAYS ARGUE LIKE THAT?
ALL THE TIME...

Don't miss ERNEST & REBECCA #1 "My Best Friend is a Germ"
coming November 2011!

Special Romantic Excerpt from CLASSICS ILLUSTRATED DELUXE #6 "The Three Musketeers"...

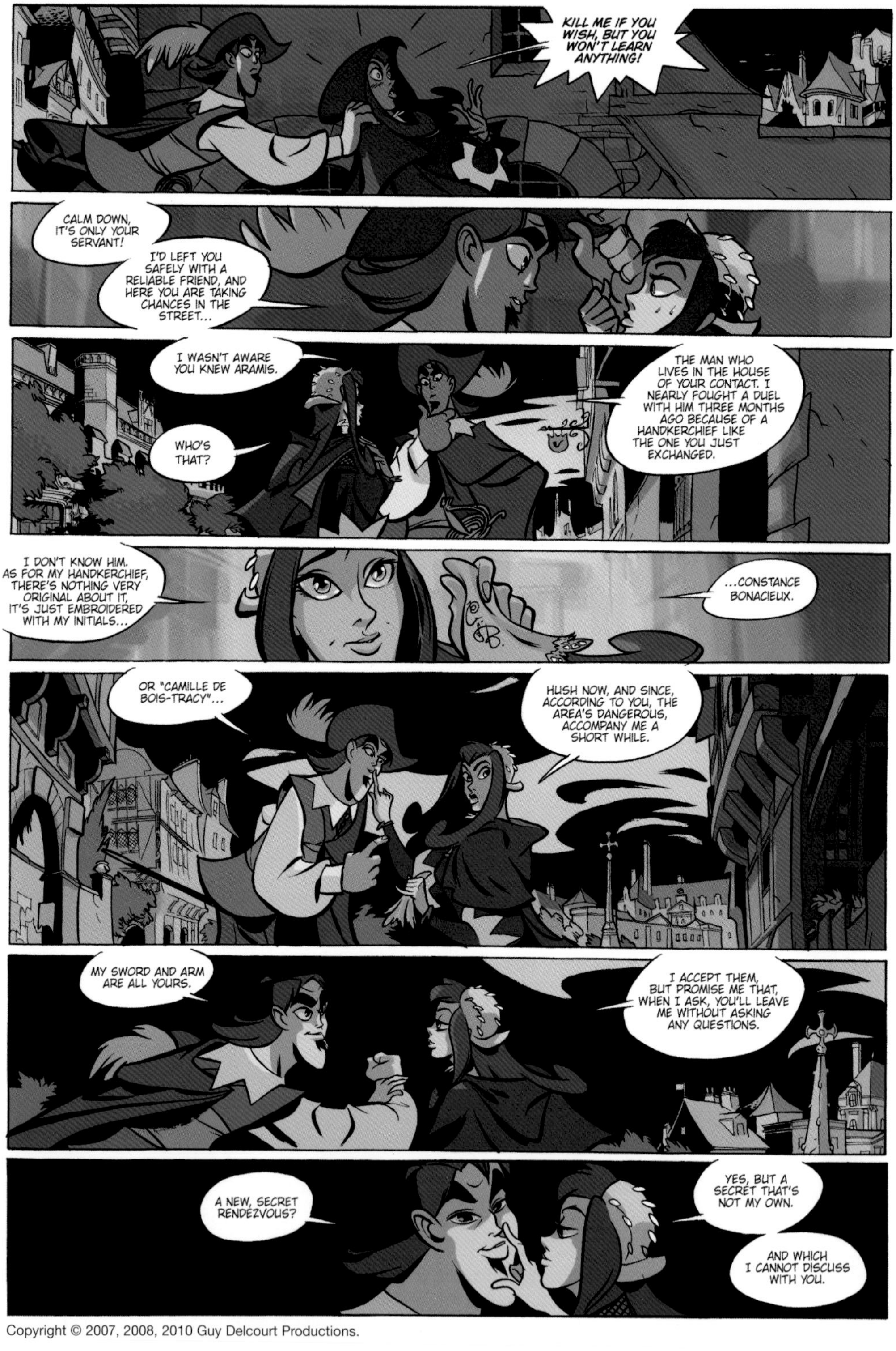
KILL ME IF YOU WISH, BUT YOU WON'T LEARN ANYTHING!
CALM DOWN, IT'S ONLY YOUR SERVANT!
I'D LEFT YOU SAFELY WITH A RELIABLE FRIEND, AND HERE YOU ARE TAKING CHANCES IN THE STREET...
I WASN'T AWARE YOU KNEW ARAMIS.
WHO'S THAT?
THE MAN WHO LIVES IN THE HOUSE OF YOUR CONTACT. I NEARLY FOUGHT A DUEL WITH HIM THREE MONTHS AGO BECAUSE OF A HANDKERCHIEF LIKE THE ONE YOU JUST EXCHANGED.
I DON'T KNOW HIM. AS FOR MY HANDKERCHIEF, THERE'S NOTHING VERY ORIGINAL ABOUT IT, IT'S JUST EMBROIDERED WITH MY INITIALS...
...CONSTANCE BONACIEUX.
OR "CAMILLE DE BOIS-TRACY"...
HUSH NOW, AND SINCE, ACCORDING TO YOU, THE AREA'S DANGEROUS, ACCOMPANY ME A SHORT WHILE.
MY SWORD AND ARM ARE ALL YOURS.
I ACCEPT THEM, BUT PROMISE ME THAT, WHEN I ASK, YOU'LL LEAVE ME WITHOUT ASKING ANY QUESTIONS.
A NEW, SECRET RENDEZVOUS?
YES, BUT A SECRET THAT'S NOT MY OWN.
AND WHICH I CANNOT DISCUSS WITH YOU.

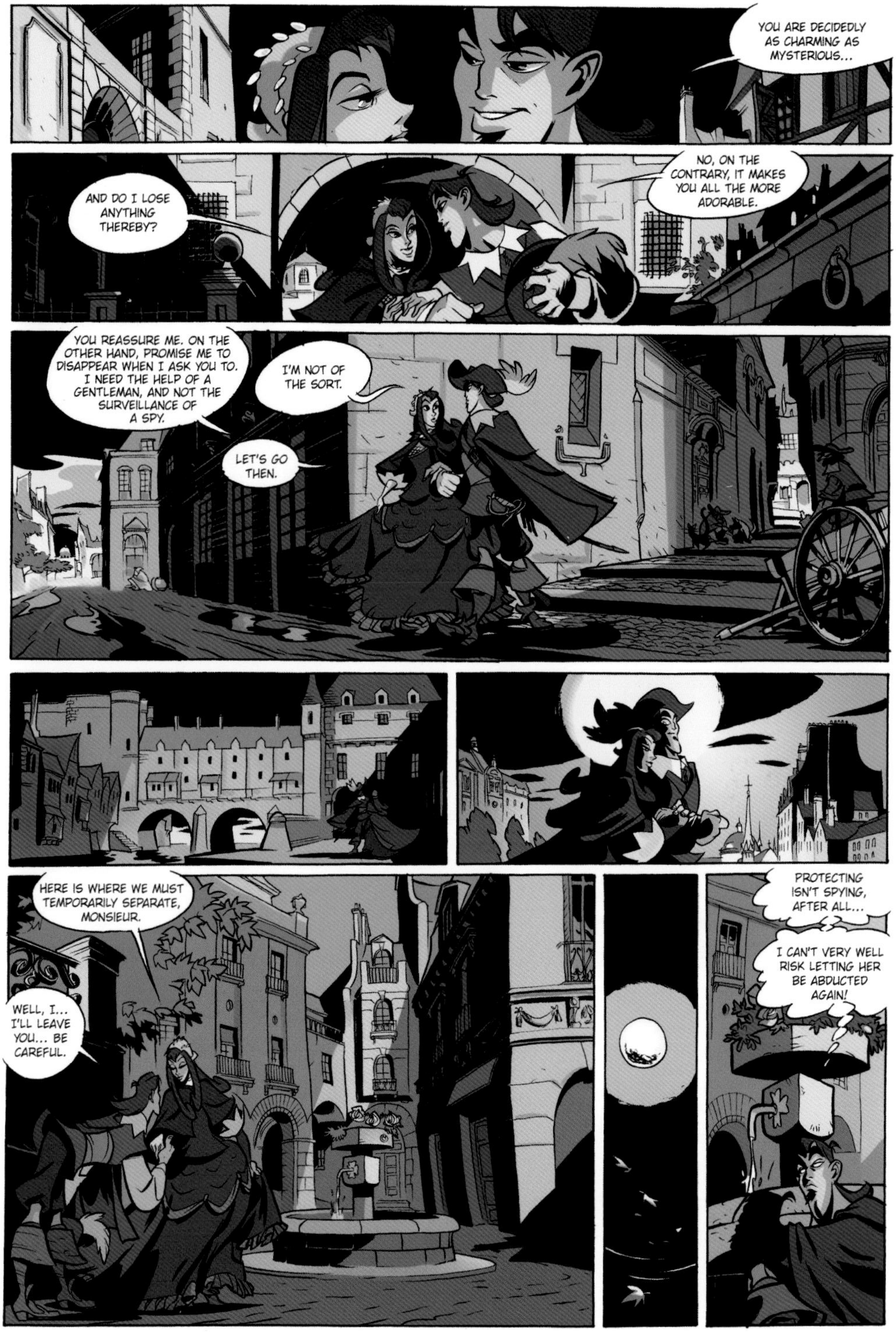
YOU ARE DECIDEDLY AS CHARMING AS MYSTERIOUS...
AND DO I LOSE ANYTHING THEREBY?
NO, ON THE CONTRARY, IT MAKES YOU ALL THE MORE ADORABLE.
YOU REASSURE ME. ON THE OTHER HAND, PROMISE ME TO DISAPPEAR WHEN I ASK YOU TO. I NEED THE HELP OF A GENTLEMAN, AND NOT THE SURVEILLANCE OF A SPY.
I'M NOT OF THE SORT.
LET'S GO THEN.
HERE IS WHERE WE MUST TEMPORARILY SEPARATE, MONSIEUR.
WELL, I... I'LL LEAVE YOU... BE CAREFUL.
PROTECTING ISN'T SPYING, AFTER ALL...
I CAN'T VERY WELL RISK LETTING HER BE ABDUCTED AGAIN!

Don't miss CLASSICS ILLUSTRATED DELUXE #6 "The Three Musketeers" available now at booksellers everywhere.

Special preview of
SYBIL THE BACKPACK FAIRY #1 “Nina”

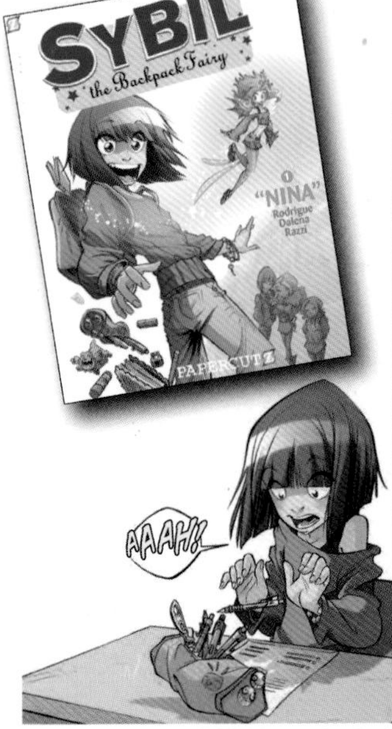
SYBIL
the Backpack Fairy
1
“NINA”
Rodrigue
Dalena
Razzi
PAPERCUTZ
AAAH!

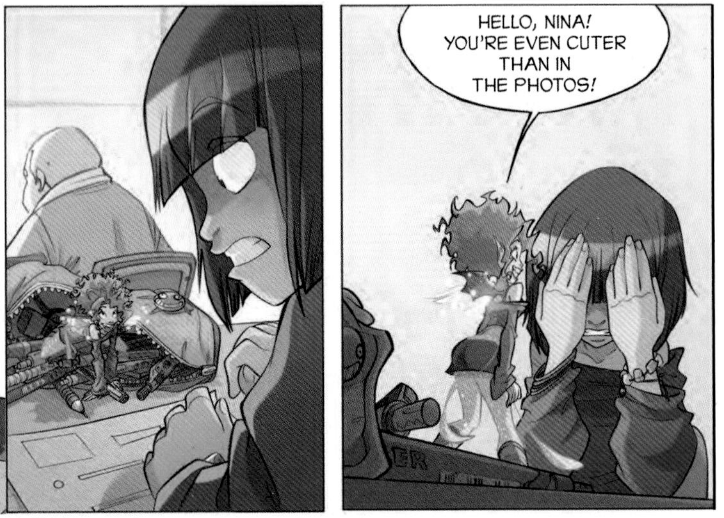
HELLO, NINA! YOU’RE EVEN CUTER THAN IN THE PHOTOS!

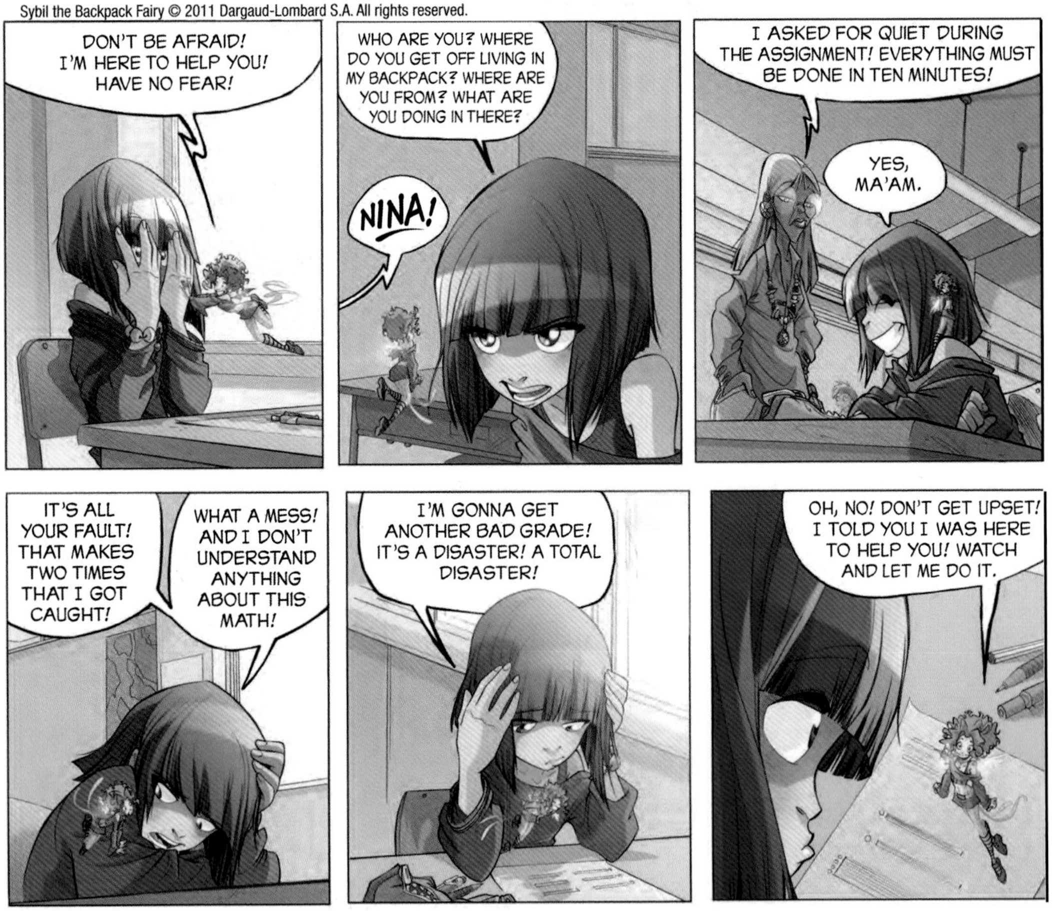
DON’T BE AFRAID! I’M HERE TO HELP YOU! HAVE NO FEAR!
WHO ARE YOU? WHERE DO YOU GET OFF LIVING IN MY BACKPACK? WHERE ARE YOU FROM? WHAT ARE YOU DOING IN THERE?
NINA!
I ASKED FOR QUIET DURING THE ASSIGNMENT! EVERYTHING MUST BE DONE IN TEN MINUTES!
YES, MA’AM.
IT’S ALL YOUR FAULT! THAT MAKES TWO TIMES THAT I GOT CAUGHT!
WHAT A MESS! AND I DON’T UNDERSTAND ANYTHING ABOUT THIS MATH!
I’M GONNA GET ANOTHER BAD GRADE! IT’S A DISASTER! A TOTAL DISASTER!
OH, NO! DON’T GET UPSET! I TOLD YOU I WAS HERE TO HELP YOU! WATCH AND LET ME DO IT.

Don’t miss SYBIL THE BACKPACK FAIRY #1 “Nina”
coming November 2011!

Emily Brontë was born in Thornton, Yorkshire, England, in 1818, the fifth of six children in a closely knit, provincial family headed by the Reverend Patrick Brontë, a Church of England clergyman, and his wife, Maria Branwell. Upon their mother's death in 1821, Maria, Elizabeth, Charlotte and Emily – the four oldest girls – were sent away to the Clergy Daughter's School. When harsh conditions at the boarding school contributed to the early deaths of their two sisters, Charlotte and Emily rejoined their father, brother Branwell, and younger sister Anne at Haworth parsonage on the Yorkshire moors. The four children had a rich fantasy life, which provided escape from the tedium of religion and relief from the poverty-stricken countryside; they concocted a fanciful world of romantic kingdoms, and recounted the exploits of their imaginary characters in a massive collection of journals, plays, poems, and stories. When they tired of inventing their own tales, the siblings delighted in poring over the creations of others – in the manifold volumes of their father's impressive library. The most solitary of the children, Emily seemed destined to forever remain at home; several stays at other boarding schools ended prematurely, when, homesick, she withdrew. In 1842, however, Emily went with Charlotte to Belgium to study languages. When they returned after a year, the two sisters opened a school in the parsonage, but did not draw a single student. Two years later, Charlotte happened upon a cache of Emily's recent poems; she immediately realized, Charlotte wrote later, that her sister's work had "a peculiar music – wild, melancholy, and elevating." At Charlotte's insistence, the three sisters compiled a collection of poems, which was released pseudonymously in 1846. Despite disappointing sales, Charlotte, Emily, and Anne were exuberant about their joint publication, and each set to work on novels. Charlotte's *Jane Eyre*, published in October 1847, was the first to appear, followed two months later by Emily's *Wuthering Heights* and Anne's *Agnes Grey*; initially, all were published under pseudonyms. The end of this remarkable family came quickly. Branwell succumbed to alcoholism in September 1848; he was followed two months later by Emily, who died of tuberculosis. Anne died quietly in July 1849. Charlotte, who fought successfully for the posthumous recognition of Emily and Anne for their works, died in 1855.

Rick Geary was born in 1946 in Kansas City, Missouri, and grew up in Wichita, Kansas. He graduated from the University of Kansas in Lawrence, where his first cartoons were published in the *University Daily Kansan*.
He began work in comics in 1977 and was for thirteen years a contributor to the Funny Pages of *National Lampoon*. His comic stories have also been published in *Heavy Metal*, Dark Horse Comics, and the DC Comics/Paradox Press Big Books. During a four-year stay in New York, his illustrations appeared regularly in *The New York Times Book Review*. His illustration work has also been seen in *MAD, Spy, Rolling Stone, The Los Angeles Times*, and *American Libraries*.
His graphic novels include three adaptations for CLASSICS ILLUSTRATED, the series *A Treasury of Victorian Murder* and the continuing series *A Treasury of XXth Century Murder*, both for NBM Publishing. In 2007, he wrote and illustrated *J. Edgar Hoover: A Graphic Biography* for Farrar, Straus, and Giroux.
Rick has received the Inkpot Award from the San Diego Comic Convention (1980), the Book and Magazine Illustration Award from the National Cartoonists Society (1994), and the Eisner Award (2007).
He and his wife Deborah live in the town of Carrizozo, New Mexico.

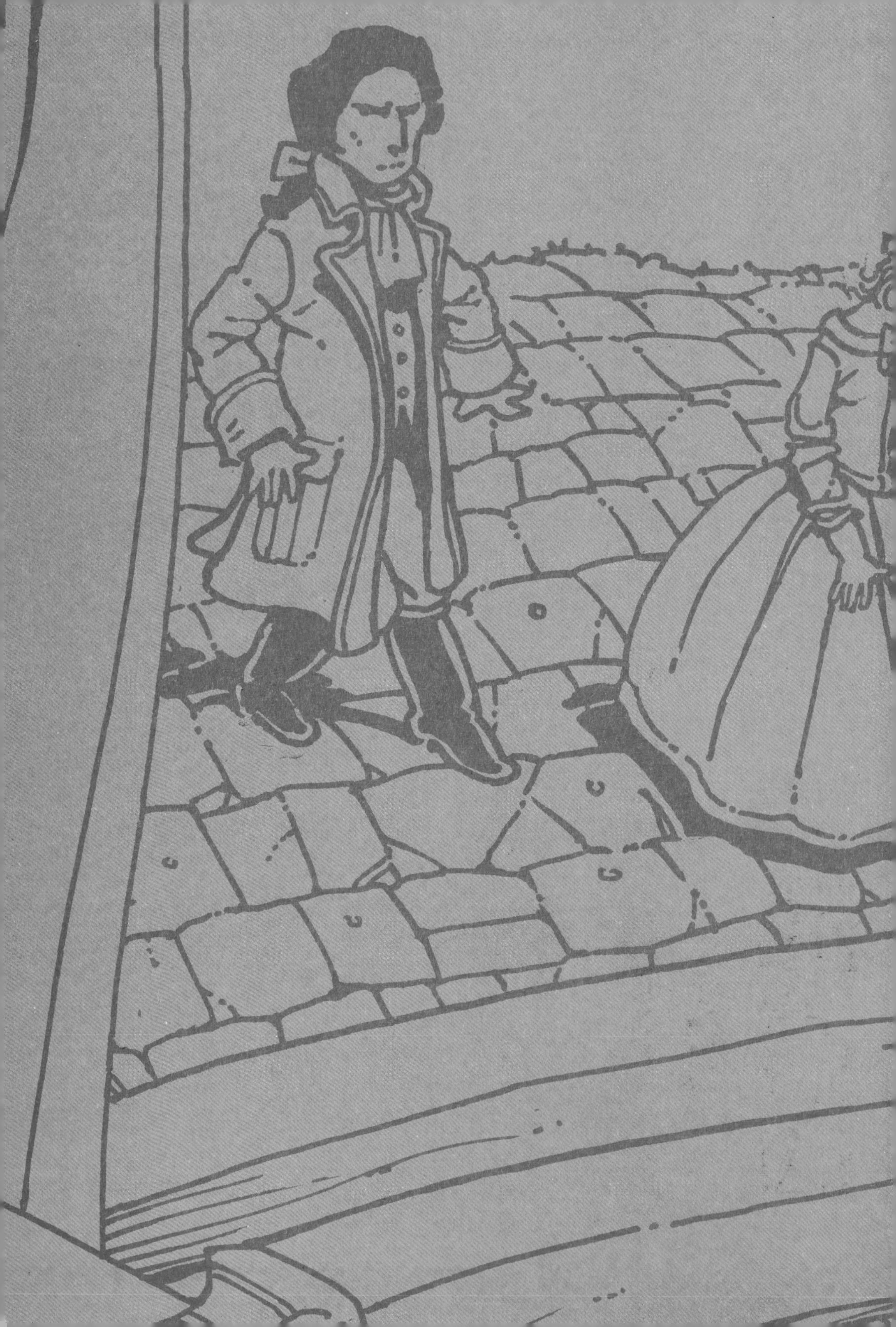